"Miss Christie at the apex of her form. To match the sheer ingenuity of Poirot's last case, you have to go back to the case that made him famous, *The Murder of Roger Ackroyd*."
—*John Barkham Reviews*

"All the familiar Christie devices—superbly drawn oddballs and ends, distracting clues, false conclusions, private moralizing—are here. *Curtain* is great diverting fun."
—*Playboy*

"Every whodunit addict will treasure *Curtain*."
—*Philadelphia Bulletin*

"Poirot . . . achieves and carries off an act not even Sherlock Holmes in his prime attained to."
—*Publishers Weekly*

"*Curtain,* suspenseful and challenging to the climax, should provide a satisfactory end to the long and entertaining Poirot saga for even the most avid of his fans."
—*King Features*

CURTAIN
was originally published by Dodd, Mead & Company, Inc.

Books by Agatha Christie

Published by POCKET BOOKS

CURTAIN

Agatha Christie

PUBLISHED BY POCKET BOOKS NEW YORK

CURTAIN

Dodd, Mead edition published 1975

POCKET BOOK edition published 1976
3rd printing......................August, 1976

This POCKET BOOK edition includes every word contained in
the original, higher-priced edition. It is printed from brand-
new plates made from completely reset, clear, easy-to-read type.
POCKET BOOK editions are published by
POCKET BOOKS,
a division of Simon & Schuster, Inc.,
A GULF+WESTERN COMPANY
630 Fifth Avenue,
New York, N.Y. 10020.
Trademarks registered in the United States
and other countries.

CURTAIN

ONE

Who is there who has not felt a sudden startled pang at reliving an old experience or feeling an old emotion?

"I have done this before . . ."

Why do those words always move one so profoundly?

That was the question I asked myself as I sat in the train watching the flat Essex landscape outside.

How long ago was it that I had taken this self-same journey? Had felt (ridiculously) that the best of life was over for me! Wounded in that war that for me would always be *the* war—the war that was wiped out now by a second and a more desperate war.

It had seemed in 1916 to young Arthur Hastings

1

that he was already old and mature. How little had I realized that, for me, life was only then beginning.

I had been journeying, though I did not know it, to meet the man whose influence over me was to shape and mould my life. Actually I had been going to stay with my old friend John Cavendish, whose mother, recently remarried, had a country house named "Styles." A pleasant renewing of old acquaintanceships, that was all I had thought it, not foreseeing that I was shortly to plunge into all the dark embroilments of a mysterious murder.

It was at Styles that I had met again that strange little man, Hercule Poirot, whom I had first come across in Belgium.

How well I remembered my amazement when I had seen the limping figure with the large moustache coming up the village street.

Hercule Poirot! Since those days he had been my dearest friend; his influence had moulded my life. In company with him, in the hunting down of yet another murderer, I had met my wife, the truest and sweetest companion any man could have had.

She lay now in Argentine soil, dying as she would have wished, with no long-drawn-out suffering or feebleness of old age. But she had left a very lonely and unhappy man behind her.'

Ah! If I could go back—live life all over again. If this could have been that day in 1916 when I first travelled to Styles . . . What changes had taken place since then! What gaps among the familiar faces. Styles itself had been sold by the Cavendishes. John Cavendish was dead, though his wife Mary (that fascinating, enigmatical creature) was still alive, living in Devonshire. Lawrence was living with his wife and children in South Africa. Changes—changes everywhere.

But one thing, strangely enough, was the same. I was going to Styles to meet Hercule Poirot.

How stupefied I had been to receive his letter, with its heading Styles Court, Styles, Essex.

I had not seen my old friend for nearly a year. The last time I had seen him I had been shocked and saddened. He was now a very old man, and almost crippled with arthritis. He had gone to Egypt in the hopes of improving his health, but had returned, so his letter told me, rather worse than better. Nevertheless, he wrote cheerfully . . .

"And does it not intrigue you, my friend, to see the address from which I write? It recalls old memories, does it not? Yes, I am here, at Styles. Figure to yourself, it is now what they call a guest house. Run by one of your so British old colonels— very 'old school tie' and 'Poona.' It is his wife, *bien entendu*, who makes it pay. She is a good manager, that one, but the tongue like vinegar, and the poor Colonel, he suffers much from it. If it were me, I would take a hatchet to her!

"I saw their advertisement in the paper, and the fancy took me to go once again to the place which

3

first was my home in this country. At my age one enjoys reliving the past.

"Then, figure to yourself, I find here a gentleman, a baronet who is a friend of the employer of your daughter. (That phrase, it sounds a little like the French exercise, does it not?)

"Immediately I conceive a plan. He wishes to induce the Franklins to come here for the summer. I in my turn will persuade you, and we shall be all together, *en famille*. It will be most agreeable. Therefore, mon cher Hastings, *dépêchez vous*, arrive with the utmost celerity. I have commanded for you a room with bath (it is modernized now, you comprehend, the dear old 'Styles') and disputed the price with Mrs. Colonel Luttrell until I have made an arrangement *très bon marche*.

"The Franklins and your charming Judith have been here for some days. It is all arranged, so make no histories. *A bientôt*. Yours always, Hercule Poirot."

The prospect was alluring, and I fell in with my old friend's wishes without demur. I had no ties and no settled home. Of my children, one boy was in the Navy, the other married and running the ranch in the Argentine. My daughter Grace was married to a soldier and was at present in India. My remaining child, Judith, was the one whom secretly I had always loved best, although I had never for one moment understood her. A queer, dark, secretive child, with a passion for keeping her own counsel, which had sometimes

4

affronted and distressed me. My wife had been more understanding. It was, she assured me, no lack of trust or confidence on Judith's part, but a kind of fierce compulsion. But she, like myself, was sometimes worried about the child. Judith's feelings, she said, were too intense, too concentrated, and her instinctive reserve deprived her of any safety valve. She had queer fits of brooding silence and a fierce, almost bitter power of partisanship. Her brains were the best of the family and we gladly fell in with her wish for a university education. She had taken her B.Sc. about a year ago, and had then taken the post of secretary to a doctor who was engaged in research work connected with tropical disease. His wife was somewhat of an invalid.

I had occasionally had qualms as to whether Judith's absorption in her work and devotion to her employer were not signs that she might be losing her heart, but the businesslike footing of their relationship assured me.

Judith was, I believed, fond of me, but she was very undemonstrative by nature, and she was often scornful and impatient of what she called my sentimental and outworn ideas. I was, frankly, a little nervous of my daughter!

At this point my meditations were interrupted by the train drawing up at the station of Styles St. Mary. That at least had not changed. Time had passed it by. It was still perched up in the midst of fields, with apparently no reason for existence.

As my taxi passed through the village, though, I realized the passage of years. Styles St. Mary was altered out of all recognition. Petrol stations, a cinema, two more inns and rows of council houses.

Presently we turned in at the gate of the Styles. Here we seemed to recede again from modern times. The park was much as I remembered it, but the drive was badly kept and much overgrown with weeds—growing up over the gravel. We turned a corner and came in view of the house. It was un-altered from the outside and badly needed a coat of paint.

As on my arrival all those years ago, there was a woman's figure stooping over one of the garden beds. My heart missed a beat. Then the figure straightened up and came towards me, and I laughed at myself. No greater contrast to the ro-bust Evelyn Howard could have been imagined.

This was a frail elderly lady with an abundance of curly white hair, pink cheeks, and a pair of cold pale blue eyes that were widely at variance with the easy geniality of her manner, which was frankly a shade too gushing for my taste.

"It'll be Captain Hastings now, won't it?" she demanded. "And me with my hands all over dirt and not able to shake hands. We're delighted to see you here—the amount we've heard about you! I must introduce myself. I'm Mrs. Luttrell. My hus-band and I bought this place in a fit of madness and have been trying to make a paying concern of it. I never thought the day would come when I'd be a hotelkeeper! But I'll warn you, Captain Hastings, I'm a very businesslike woman. I pile up the extras all I know how."

We both laughed as though at an excellent joke, but it occurred to me that what Mrs. Luttrell had just said was in all probability the literal truth. Behind the veneer of her charming old-lady manner, I caught a glimpse of flintlike hardness.

Although Mrs. Luttrell occasionally affected a faint brogue, she had no Irish blood. It was a mere affectation.

I inquired after my friend.

"Ah, poor little M. Poirot. The way he's been looking forward to your coming. It would melt a heart of stone. Terribly sorry I am for him, suffering the way he does."

We were walking towards the house and she was peeling off her gardening gloves.

"And your pretty daughter, too," she went on. "What a lovely girl she is. We all admire her tremendously. But I'm old-fashioned, you know, and it seems to me a shame and a sin that a girl like that, that ought to be going to parties and dancing with young men, should spend her time cutting up rabbits and bending over a microscope all day. Leave that sort of thing to the frumps, I say."

"Where is Judith?" I asked. "Is she somewhere about?"

Mrs. Luttrell made what children call "a face."

"Ah, the poor girl! She's cooped up in that stu-

7

dio place down at the bottom of the garden. Dr. Franklin rents it from me and he's had it all fitted up. Hutches of guinea pigs he's got there, the poor creatures, and mice and rabbits. I'm not sure that I like all this science, Captain Hastings. Ah, here's my husband."

Colonel Luttrell had just come round the corner of the house. He was a very tall, attenuated old man with a cadaverous face, mild blue eyes and a habit of irresolutely tugging at his little white moustache.

He had a vague, rather nervous manner.

"Ah, George, here's Captain Hastings arrived."

Colonel Luttrell shook hands. "You came by the five—er—forty, eh?"

"What else should he have come by?" said Mrs. Luttrell sharply. "And what does it matter anyway? Take him up and show him his room, George. And then maybe he'd like to go straight to M. Poirot—or would you rather have tea first?"

I assured her that I did not want tea and would prefer to go and greet my friend.

Colonel Luttrell said, "Right. Come along. I expect—er—they'll have taken your things up already—eh, Daisy?"

Mrs. Luttrell said tartly, "That's your business, George. I've been gardening. I can't see to everything."

"No, no, of course not. I—I'll see to it, my dear."

I followed him up the front steps. In the doorway we encountered a grey-haired man, slightly built, who was hurrying out with a pair of field glasses. He limped, and had a boyish, eager face. He said, stammering slightly, "There's a pair of n-nesting birds down by the sycamore."

As we went into the hall, Luttrell said, "That's Stephen Norton. Nice fellow. Crazy about birds."

In the hall itself, a very big man was standing by the table. He had obviously just finished telephoning. Looking up, he said, "I'd like to hang, draw and quarter all contractors and builders. Never get anything done right, curse 'em."

His wrath was so comical and so rueful that we both laughed. I felt attracted at once towards the man. He was very good-looking, though a man well over fifty, with a deeply tanned face. He looked as though he had led an out-of-door life, and he looked, too, the type of man that is becoming more and more rare—an Englishman of the old school, straightforward, fond of out-of-door life, and the kind of man who can command.

I was hardly surprised when Colonel Luttrell introduced him as Sir William Boyd Carrington. He had been, I knew, governor of a province in India, where he had been a signal success. He was also renowned as a first-class shot and big game hunter. The sort of man, I reflected sadly, that we no longer seemed to breed in these degenerate days.

"Aha," he said, "I'm glad to meet in the flesh that famous personage *mon ami* Hastings." He laughed. "The dear old Belgian fellow talks about

9

you a lot, you know. And then, of course, we've got your daughter here. She's a fine girl."

"I don't suppose Judith talks about me much," I said, smiling.

"No, no, far too modern. These girls nowadays always seem embarrassed at having to admit to a father or mother at all."

"Parents," I said, "are practically a disgrace."

He laughed. "Oh, well—I don't suffer that way. I've no children, worse luck. Your Judith is a very good-looking wench, but terribly highbrow. I find it rather alarming." He picked up the telephone receiver again. "Hope you don't mind, Luttrell, if I start damning your exchange to hell. I'm not a patient man."

"Do 'em good," said Luttrell.

He led the way upstairs and I followed him. He took me along the left wing of the house to a door at the end, and I realized that Poirot had chosen for me the room I had occupied before.

There were changes here. As I walked along the corridor, some of the doors were open and I saw that the old-fashioned large bedrooms had been partitioned off so as to make several smaller ones.

My own room, which had not been large, was unaltered save for the installation of hot and cold water, and part of it had been partitioned off to make a small bathroom. It was furnished in a cheap modern style which rather disappointed me. I should have preferred a style more nearly approximating the architecture of the house itself.

My luggage was in my room and the Colonel explained that Poirot's room was exactly opposite. He was about to take me there when a sharp cry of "George" echoed up from the hall below.

Colonel Luttrell started like a nervous horse. His hand went to his lips.

"I—I—sure you're all right? Ring for what you want—"

"*George.*"

"Coming, my dear, coming."

He hurried off down the corridor. I stood for a moment looking after him. Then, with my heart beating slightly faster, I crossed the corridor and rapped on the door of Poirot's room.

TWO

Nothing is so sad, in my opinion, as the devastation wrought by age.

My poor friend. I have described him many times. Now to convey to you the difference. Crippled with arthritis, he propelled himself about in a wheelchair. His once plump frame had fallen in. He was a thin little man now. His face was lined and wrinkled. His moustache and hair, it is true, were still of a jet-black colour, but candidly, though I would not for the world have hurt his feelings by saying so to him, this was a mistake. There comes a moment when hair dye is only too painfully obvious. There had been a time when I had been surprised to learn that the blackness of Poirot's hair came out of a bottle. But now the theatricality was apparent and merely created the

13

impression that he wore a wig and had adorned his upper lip to amuse the children!

Only his eyes were the same as ever, shrewd and twinkling, and now—yes, undoubtedly—softened with emotion:

"Ah, *mon ami* Hastings—*mon ami* Hastings . . ."

I bent my head and, as was his custom, he embraced me warmly.

"Mon ami Hastings!"

He leaned back, surveying me with his head a little on one side.

"Yes, just the same—the straight back, the broad shoulders, the grey of the hair—*très distingué*. You know, my friend, you have worn well. *Les femmes*, they still take an interest in you? Yes?"

"Really, Poirot," I protested. "Must you—"

"But I assure you, my friend, it is a test—it is the test. When the very young girls come and talk to you kindly, oh, so kindly—it is the end! 'The poor old man,' they say; 'we must be nice to him. It must be so awful to be like that.' But you, Hastings—*vous êtes encore jeune*. For you there are still possibilities. That is right, twist your moustache, hunch your shoulders—I see it is as I say— you would not look so self-conscious otherwise."

I burst out laughing.

"You really are the limit, Poirot. And how are you yourself?"

"Me," said Poirot with a grimace. "I am a wreck. I am a ruin. I cannot walk. I am crippled and twisted. Mercifully I can still feed myself, but otherwise I have to be attended to like a baby. Put to bed, washed and dressed. *Enfin,* it is not amusing, that. Mercifully, though the outside decays, the core is still sound."

"Yes, indeed. The best heart in the world."

"The heart? Perhaps. I was not referring to the heart. The brain, *mon cher,* is what I mean by the core. My brain, it still functions magnificently."

I could at least perceive clearly that no deterioration of the brain in the direction of modesty had taken place.

"And you like it here?" I asked.

Poirot shrugged his shoulders.

"It suffices. It is not, you comprehend, the Ritz. No, indeed. The room I was in when I first came here was both small and inadequately furnished. I moved to this one with no increase of price. Then, the cooking, it is English at its worst. Those Brussels sprouts so enormous, so hard, that the English like so much. The potatoes boiled and either hard or falling to pieces. The vegetables that taste of water, water, and again water. The complete absence of the salt and pepper in any dish—" He paused expressively.

"It sounds terrible," I said.

"I do not complain," said Poirot, and proceeded to do so. "And there is also the modernization, so called. The bathrooms, the taps everywhere, and what comes out of them? Lukewarm water, *mon ami*, at most hours of the day. And the towels, so thin, so meagre!"

"There is something to be said for the old days," I said thoughtfully. I remembered the clouds of steam which had gushed from the hot tap of the one bathroom Styles had originally possessed, one of those bathrooms in which an immense bath with mahogany sides had reposed proudly in the middle of the bathroom floor. Remembered, too, the immense bath towels, and the frequent shining brass cans of boiling hot water that stood in one's old-fashioned basin.

"But one must not complain," said Poirot again. "I am content to suffer—for a good cause."

A sudden thought struck me.

"I say, Poirot, you're not—er—hard up, are you? I know the war hit investments very badly—"

Poirot reassured me quickly.

"No, no, my friend. I am in most comfortable circumstances. Indeed, I am rich. It is not the economy that brings me here."

"Then that's all right," I said.

I went on:

"I think I can understand your feeling. As one gets on, one tends more and more to revert to the old days. One tries to recapture old emotions. I find it painful to be here, in a way, and yet it brings back to me a hundred old thoughts and emotions that I'd quite forgotten I ever felt. I daresay you feel the same."

"Not in the least. I do not feel like that at all."

"They were good days," I said sadly.

"You may speak for yourself, Hastings. For me, my arrival at Styles St. Mary was a sad and painful time. I was a refugee, wounded, exiled from home and country, existing by charity in a foreign land. No, it was not gay. I did not know then that England would come to be my home and that I should find happiness here."

"I had forgotten that," I admitted.

"Precisely. You attribute always to others the sentiments that you yourself experience. Hastings was happy—everybody was happy!"

"No, no," I protested, laughing.

"And in any case it is not true," continued Poirot; "you look back, you say, the tears rising in your eyes, 'Oh, the happy days. Then I was young.' But indeed, my friend, you were not so happy as you think. You had recently been severely wounded, you were fretting at being no longer fit for active service, you had just been depressed beyond words by your sojourn in a dreary convalescent home, and as far as I remember, you proceeded to complicate matters by falling in love with two women at the same time."

I laughed and flushed.

"What a memory you have, Poirot."

"Ta ta ta—I remember now the melancholy sigh you heaved as you murmured fatuities about two lovely women."

"Do you remember what you said? You said, 'And neither of them is for you! Never mind. Console yourself, *mon ami*. We may hunt together again and then—' "

I stopped. For Poirot and I had gone hunting again to France and it was there that I had met the one woman . . .

Gently my friend patted my arm.

"I know, Hastings, I know. The wound is still fresh. But do not dwell on it, do not look back. Instead look forward."

I made a gesture of disgust.

"Look forward? What is there to look forward to?"

"*Eh bien*, my friend, there is work to be done."

"Work? Where?"

"Here."

I stared at him.

"Just now," said Poirot, "you asked me why I had come here. You may not have observed that I gave you no answer. I will give you the answer now. I am here to hunt down a murderer."

I stared at him with even more astonishment. For a moment I thought he was rambling.

"You really mean that?"

"But certainly I mean it. For what other reason did I urge you to join me? My limbs, they are no longer active, but my brain, as I told you, is unimpaired. My rule, remember, has been always the same—sit back and think. That I still can do. In fact, it is the only thing possible to me. For the more active side of the campaign I shall have with me my invaluable Hastings."

"You really mean it?" I gasped.

"Of course I mean it. You and I, Hastings, *are going hunting once again.*"

It took me some minutes to grasp that Poirot was really in earnest.

Fantastic though his statement sounded, I had no reason to doubt his judgment.

With a slight smile he said, "At last you are convinced. At first you imagined, did you not, that I had the softening of the brain?"

"No, no," I said hastily. "Only this seems such an unlikely place."

"Ah, you think so?"

"Of course I haven't seen all the people yet—"

"Whom have you seen?"

"Just the Luttrells, and a man called Norton, seems an inoffensive chap, and Boyd Carrington —I must say I took the greatest fancy to him."

Poirot nodded.

"Well, Hastings, I will tell you this. When you have seen the rest of the household, my statement will seem to you just as impossible as it is now."

"Who else is there?"

"The Franklins—Doctor and Mrs.—the hospital nurse who attends to Mrs. Franklin, your daughter Judith. Then there is a man called Allerton, something of a lady-killer, and a Miss Cole, a woman of about thirty-five. They are all, let me tell you, very nice people."

"And one of them is a murderer?"

"And one of them is a murderer."

"But why—how—why should you think—?"

I found it hard to frame my questions; they tumbled over each other.

"Calm yourself, Hastings. Let us begin from the beginning. Reach me, I pray you, that small box from the bureau. *Bien*. And now the key—so—"

Unlocking the dispatch case, he took from it a mass of typescript and newspaper clippings.

"You can study these at your leisure, Hastings. For the moment I should not bother with the newspaper cuttings. They are merely the press accounts of various tragedies, occasionally inaccurate, sometimes suggestive. To give you an idea of the cases, I suggest that you should read through the précis I have made."

Deeply interested, I started reading.

CASE A. ETHERINGTON

Leonard Etherington. Unpleasant habits—took drugs and also drank. A peculiar and sadistic character. Wife young and attractive. Desperately unhappy with him. Etherington died, apparently of food poisoning. Doctor not satisfied. As a result of autopsy, death discovered to be due to arsenical poisoning. Supply of weed killer in the house, but ordered a long time previously. Mrs. Etherington arrested and charged with murder. She had recently been friends with a man in Civil Service returning to India. No suggestion of actual infidelity, but evidence of deep sympathy between them. Young man had since become engaged to be married to girl he met on voyage out. Some doubt as to whether letter telling Mrs. Etherington of this fact was received by her after or before her husband's death. She herself says before. Evidence against her mainly circumstantial, absence of another likely suspect and accident highly unlikely. Great sympathy felt with her at trial owing to husband's character and the bad treatment she had received from him. Judge's summing up was in her favour, stressing that verdict must be beyond any reasonable doubt.

Mrs. Etherington was acquitted. General opinion, however, was that she was guilty. Her life afterwards very difficult owing to friends, etc., cold-shouldering her. She died as a result of taking an overdose of sleeping draught two years after the trial. Verdict of accidental death returned at inquest.

CASE B. SHARPLES

Elderly spinster. An invalid. Difficult, suffering much pain. She was looked after by her niece, Freda Clay. Miss Sharples died as a result of an overdose of morphia. Freda Clay admitted an error, saying that her aunt's sufferings were so bad that she could not stand it and gave her more morphia to ease the pain. Opinion of police that act was deliberate, not a mistake, but they considered evidence insufficient on which to prosecute.

CASE C. RIGGS

Edward Riggs, agricultural labourer. Suspected his wife of infidelity with their lodger, Ben Craig. Craig and Mrs. Riggs found shot. Shots proved to be from Riggs's gun. Riggs gave himself up to the police, said he supposed he must have done it, but couldn't remember. His mind went blank, he said. Riggs sentenced to death, sentence afterwards commuted to penal servitude for life.

CASE D. BRADLEY

Derek Bradley. Was carrying on an intrigue with a girl. His wife discovered this; she threatened to kill him. Bradley died of potassium cyanide administered in his beer. Mrs. Bradley arrested and tried for murder. Broke down under cross-examination. Convicted and hanged.

CASE E. LITCHFIELD

Elderly tyrant, Matthew Litchfield. Four daughters at home, not allowed any pleasures or money to spend. One evening on returning home, he was attacked outside his side door and killed by a blow on the head. Later, after police investigation, his eldest daughter, Margaret, walked into the police station and gave herself up for her father's murder. She did it, she said, in order that her younger sisters might be able to have a life of their own before it was too late. Litchfield left a large fortune. Margaret Litchfield was adjudged insane and committed to Broadmoor, but died shortly afterwards.

I read carefully, but with a growing bewilderment. Finally I put the paper down and looked inquiringly at Poirot.

"Well, *mon ami*?"

"I remember the Bradley case," I said slowly. "I read about it at the time. She was a very goodlooking woman."

Poirot nodded.

"But you must enlighten me. What is all this about?"

"Tell me first what it amounts to in your eyes."

I was rather puzzled.

"What you gave me was an account of five different murders. They all occurred in different places and amongst different classes of people. Moreover, there seems no superficial resemblance between them. That is to say, one was a case of jealousy, one was an unhappy wife seeking to get rid of her husband, another had money for a motive, another was, you might say, unselfish in aim since the murderer did not try to escape punishment, and the fifth was frankly brutal, probably committed under the influence of drink."

I paused and said doubtfully:

"Is there something in common between them all that I have missed?"

"No, no, you have been very accurate in your summing up. The only point that you might have mentioned but did not, was the fact that in none of those cases did any real *doubt* exist."

"I don't think I understand?"

"Mrs. Etherington, for instance, was acquitted. But everybody, nevertheless, was quite certain that she did it. Freda Clay was not openly accused, but no one thought of any alternative solution of the crime. Riggs stated that he did not remember killing his wife and her lover, but there was never any question of anybody else having done so. Margaret Litchfield confessed. In each case, you see, Hastings, there was one clear suspect and no other."

I wrinkled my brow.

"Yes, that is true—but I don't see what particular inferences you draw from that."

"Ah, but you see, I am coming to a fact that you do not know as yet. Supposing, Hastings, that in each of these cases that I have outlined, there was one alien note common to them all?"

"What do you mean?"

Poirot said slowly:

"I intend, Hastings, to be very careful in what I say. Let me put it this way. There is a certain person—X. In none of these cases did X (apparently) have any motive in doing away with the victim. In one case, as far as I have been able to find out, X was actually two hundred miles away when the crime was committed. Nevertheless, I will tell you this. X was on intimate terms with Etherington, X lived for a time in the same village as Riggs, X was acquainted with Mrs. Bradley. I have a snap of X and Freda Clay walking together in the street, and X was near the house when old Matthew Litchfield died. What do you say to that?"

I stared at him. I said slowly:

"Yes, it's a bit too much. Coincidence might account for two cases, or even three, but five is a bit too thick. There must, unlikely as it seems, be some connection between these different murders."

"You assume, then, what I have assumed?"

"That X is the murderer? Yes."

"In that case, Hastings, you will be willing to go with me one step further. Let me tell you this. X *is in this house.*"

"Here? At Styles?"

"At Styles. What is the logical inference to be drawn from that?"

I knew what was coming as I said:

"Go on—say it."

Hercule Poirot said gravely:

"A murder will shortly be committed here— *here.*"

THREE

For a moment or two I stared at Poirot in dismay, then I reacted.

"No, it won't," I said. "You'll prevent that."

Poirot threw me an affectionate glance.

"My loyal friend. How much I appreciate your faith in me. *Tout de même,* I am not sure if it is justified in this case."

"Nonsense. Of course you can stop it."

Poirot's voice was grave as he said:

"Reflect a minute, Hastings. One can catch a murderer, yes. But how does one proceed to stop a murder?"

"Well, you—you—well, I mean—if you know beforehand—"

I paused rather feebly—for suddenly I saw the difficulties.

27

Poirot said:

"You see? It is not so simple. There are, in fact, only three methods. The first is to warn the victim. To put the victim on his or her guard. That does not always succeed, for it is unbelievably difficult to convince some people that they are in grave danger—possibly from someone near and dear to them. They are indignant and refuse to believe. The second course is to warn the murderer. To say, in language that is only slightly veiled: '*I know your intentions*. If so-and-so dies, my friend, *you* will most surely hang.' That succeeds more often than the first method, but even there it is likely to fail. For a murderer, my friend, is more conceited than any creature on this earth. A murderer is always more clever than anyone else—no one will ever suspect him or her—the police will be utterly baffled, et cetera. Therefore he (or she) goes ahead just the same, and all you can have is the satisfaction of hanging them afterwards." He paused and said thoughtfully:

"Twice in my life I have warned a murderer— once in Egypt, once elsewhere. In each case, the criminal was determined to kill . . . It may be so here."

"You said there was a third method," I reminded him.

"Ah yes. For that one needs the utmost ingenuity. You have to guess exactly how and when the blow is timed to fall and you have to be ready to step in at the exact psychological moment. You

28

have to catch the murderer, if not quite red-handed, then guilty of the intention beyond any possible doubt.

"And that, my friend," went on Poirot, "is, I can assure you, a matter of great difficulty and delicacy, and I would not for a moment guarantee its success! I may be conceited, but I am not so conceited as *that*."

"Which method do you propose to try here?"

"Possibly all three. The first is the most difficult."

"Why? I should have thought it the easiest."

"Yes, if you know the intended victim. But do you not realize, Hastings, that here I do not know the victim?"

"What?"

I gave vent to the exclamation without reflecting. Then the difficulties of the position began to dawn on me. There was, there must be, some link connecting this series of crimes, but we did not know what that link was. The motive, the vitally important motive, was missing. And without knowing that, we could not tell who was threatened.

Poirot nodded as he saw by my face that I was realizing the difficulties of the situation.

"You see, my friend, it is not so easy."

"No," I said. "I see that. You have so far been able to find no connection between these varying cases?"

Poirot shook his head.

"Nothing."

I reflected again. In the A.B.C. crimes, we had to

deal with what purported to be an alphabetical series, though in actuality it had turned out to be something very different.

I asked:

"There is, you are quite sure, no far-fetched financial motive—nothing, for instance, like you found in the case of Evelyn Carlisle?"

"No. You may be quite sure, my dear Hastings, that financial gain is the first thing for which I look."

That was true enough. Poirot has always been completely cynical about money.

I thought again. A vendetta of some kind? That was more in accordance with the facts. But even there, there seemed a lack of any connecting link. I recalled a story I had read of a series of purposeless murders—the clue being that the victims had happened to serve as members of a jury, and the crimes had been committed by a man whom they had condemned. It struck me that something of that kind would meet this case. I am ashamed to say that I kept the idea to myself. It would have been such a feather in my cap if I could go to Poirot with the solution.

Instead I asked:

"And now tell me, who is X?"

To my intense annoyance Poirot shook his head very decidedly.

"That, my friend, I do not tell."

"Nonsense. Why not?"

Poirot's eyes twinkled.

"Because, *mon cher*, you are still the same old Hastings. You have still the speaking countenance. I do not wish, you see, that you should sit staring at X with your mouth hanging open, your face saying plainly: 'This—this that I am looking at is a murderer.'"

"You might give me credit for a little dissimulation at need."

"When you try to dissimulate, it is worse. No, no, *mon ami*, we must be very incognito, you and I. Then, when we pounce, we pounce."

"You obstinate old devil," I said. "I've a good mind to—"

I broke off as there was a tap on the door. Poirot called, "Come in," and my daughter Judith entered.

I should like to describe Judith, but I've always been a poor hand at descriptions.

Judith is tall, she holds her head high, she has level dark brows and a very lovely line of cheek and jaw—severe in its austerity. She is grave and slightly scornful, and to my mind there has always hung about her a suggestion of tragedy.

Judith didn't come and kiss me—she is not that kind. She just smiled at me and said, "Hullo, Father."

Her smile was shy and a little embarrassed, but it made me feel that in spite of her undemonstrativeness she was pleased to see me.

"Well," I said, feeling foolish as I so often do with the younger generation, "I've got here."

31

"Very clever of you, darling," said Judith.

"I describe to him," said Poirot, "the cooking."

"Is it very bad?" asked Judith.

"You should not have to ask that, my child. Is it that you think of nothing but the test tubes and the microscopes? Your middle finger, it is stained with methylene blue. It is not a good thing for your husband if you take no interest in his stomach."

"I daresay I shan't have a husband."

"Certainly you will have a husband. What did the *bon Dieu* create you for?"

"Many things, I hope," said Judith.

"*Le mariage* first of all."

"Very well," said Judith. "You shall find me a nice husband and I will look after his stomach very carefully."

"She laughs at me," said Poirot. "Someday she will know how wise old men are."

There was another tap on the door and Dr. Franklin entered. He was a tall, angular young man of thirty-five, with a decided jaw, reddish hair, and bright blue eyes. He was the most ungainly man I had ever known, and was always knocking into things in an absent-minded way.

He cannoned into the screen round Poirot's chair and half turning his head murmured "I beg your pardon" to it automatically.

I wanted to laugh, but Judith, I noted, remained quite grave. I suppose she was quite used to that sort of thing.

32

"You remember my father," said Judith.

Dr. Franklin started, shied nervously, screwed up his eyes and peered at me, then stuck out a hand, saying awkwardly:

"Of course, of course, how are you? I heard you were coming down."

He turned to Judith.

"I say, do you think we need change? If not, we might go on a bit after dinner. If we got a few more of those slides prepared—"

"No," said Judith. "I want to talk to my father."

"Oh yes. Oh, of course." Suddenly he smiled, an apologetic boyish smile. "I am sorry—I get so awfully wrapped up in a thing. It's quite unpardonable—makes me so selfish. Do forgive me."

The clock struck and Franklin glanced at it hurriedly.

"Good Lord, is it as late as that? I shall get into trouble. Promised Barbara I'd read to her before dinner."

He grinned at us both and hurried out, colliding with the doorpost as he went out.

"How is Mrs. Franklin?" I asked.

"The same and rather more so," said Judith.

"It's very sad her being such an invalid," I said.

"It's maddening for a doctor," said Judith. "Doctors like healthy people."

"How hard you young people are!" I exclaimed.

Judith said coldly:

"I was just stating a fact."

"Nevertheless," said Poirot, "the good doctor hurries to read to her."

"Very stupid," said Judith. "That nurse of hers can read to her perfectly well if she wants to be read to. Personally I should loathe anyone reading aloud to *me*."

"Well, well, tastes differ," I said.

"She's a very stupid woman," said Judith.

"Now there, *mon enfant*," said Poirot, "I do not agree with you."

"She never reads anything but the cheapest kind of novel. She takes no interest in his work. She doesn't keep abreast of current thought. She just talks about her health to everyone who will listen."

"I still maintain," said Poirot, "that she uses her grey cells in ways that you, my child, know nothing about."

"She's a very feminine sort of woman," said Judith. "She coos and purrs. I expect you like 'em like that, Uncle Hercule."

"Not at all," I said. "He likes them large and flamboyant and Russian for choice."

"So that is how you give me away, Hastings? Your father, Judith, has always had a penchant for auburn hair. It has landed him in trouble many a time."

Judith smiled at us both indulgently. She said:

"What a funny couple you are."

She turned away and I rose.

"I must get unpacked, and I might have a bath before dinner."

Poirot pressed a little bell within reach of his hand and a minute or two later his valet attendant entered. I was surprised to find that the man was a stranger.

"Why! Where's Georges?"

Poirot's valet, Georges, had been with him for many years.

"Georges has returned to his family. His father is ill. I hope he will come back to me sometime. In the meantime," he smiled at the new valet, "Curtiss looks after me."

Curtiss smiled back respectfully. He was a big man with a bovine rather stupid face.

As I went out of the door, I noted that Poirot was carefully locking up the dispatch case with the papers inside it.

My mind in a whirl, I crossed the passage to my own room.

FOUR

I went down to dinner that night feeling that the whole of life had become suddenly unreal.

Once or twice, while dressing, I had asked myself if possibly Poirot had imagined the whole thing. After all, the dear old chap was an old man now and sadly broken in health. He himself might declare his brain was as sound as ever—but in point of fact, was it? His whole life had been spent in tracking down crime. Would it really be surprising if, in the end, he was to fancy crimes where no crimes were? His enforced inaction must have fretted him sorely. What more likely than that he should invent for himself a new manhunt? Wishful thinking—a perfectly reasonable neurosis. He had selected a number of publicly reported happenings, and had read into them something that was not there—a shadowy figure behind them—a mad mass murderer. In all probability Mrs. Etherington had really killed her husband, the labourer had shot his wife, a young woman had given her old aunt an overdose of morphia, a jealous wife had polished off her husband as she had threatened to do, and a crazy spinster had really committed the murder for which she had subsequently given herself up. In fact these crimes were exactly what they seemed!

Against that view (surely the common-sense one) I could only set my own inherent belief in Poirot's acumen.

Poirot said that a murder had been arranged. For the second time Styles was to house a crime.

Time would prove or disprove that assertion, but if it were true, it behooved us to forestall that happening.

And Poirot knew the identity of the murderer, which I did not.

The more I thought about that, the more annoyed I became! Really, frankly, it was damned cheek of Poirot! He wanted my cooperation and yet he refused to take me into his confidence!

Why? There was the reason he gave—surely a most inadequate one! I was tired of this silly joking about my "speaking countenance." I could keep a secret as well as anyone. Poirot has always persisted in the humiliating belief that I am a transparent character and that anyone can read what is passing in my mind. He tries to soften the blow sometimes by attributing it to my beautiful and honest character, which abhors all form of deceit!

Of course, I reflected, if the whole thing was a chimera of Poirot's imagination, his reticence was easily explained.

I had come to no conclusion by the time the gong sounded, and I went down to dinner with an open mind, but with an alert eye, for the detection of Poirot's mythical X.

For the moment I would accept everything that Poirot had said as gospel truth. There was a person under this roof who had already killed five times and who was preparing to kill again. *Who was it?*

In the drawing room before we went in to dinner I was introduced to Miss Cole and Major Allerton. The former was a tall, still handsome woman of thirty-three or -four. Major Allerton I instinctively disliked. He was a good-looking man in the early forties, broad-shouldered, bronzed of face, with an easy way of talking, most of what he said holding a double implication. He had the pouches under his eyes that come with a dissipated way of life. I suspected him of racketing around, of gambling, of drinking hard, and of being first and last a womanizer.

Old Colonel Luttrell, I saw, did not much like him either, and Boyd Carrington was also rather stiff in his manner towards him. Allerton's success was with the women of the party. Mrs. Luttrell twittered to him delightedly, while he flattered her lazily and with a hardly concealed impertinence. I was also annoyed to see that Judith, too, seemed to enjoy his company and was exerting herself far more than usual to talk to him. Why the worst type of man can always be relied upon to please and interest the nicest of women has long been a problem beyond me. I knew instinctively that Allerton was a rotter—and nine men out of ten would have agreed with me. Whereas nine women or possibly the whole ten would have fallen for him immediately.

As we sat down at the dinner table and plates of white gluey liquid were set before us, I let my eyes rove round the table while I summed up the possibilities.

If Poirot were right and retained his clearness of brain unimpaired, one of these people was a dangerous murderer—and probably a lunatic as well.

Poirot had not actually said so, but I presumed that X was probably a man. Which of these men was it likely to be?

Surely not old Colonel Luttrell, with his indecision and his general air of feebleness. Norton, the man whom I had met rushing out of the house with field glasses? It seemed unlikely. He appeared to be a pleasant fellow, rather ineffective and lacking in vitality. Of course, I told myself, many murderers have been small insignificant men —driven to assert themselves by crime for that very reason. They resented being passed over and ignored. Norton might be a murderer of this type.

But there was his fondness for birds. I have always believed that a love of nature was essentially a healthy sign in a man.

Boyd Carrington? Out of the question. A man with a name known all over the world. A fine sportsman, an administrator, a man universally liked and looked up to. Franklin I also dismissed. I knew how Judith respected and admired him.

Major Allerton now. I dwelt on him appraisingly. A nasty fellow if I ever saw one! The sort of fellow who would skin his grandmother. And all glossed over with this superficial charm of manner. He was talking now—telling a story of his own discomfiture and making everybody laugh with his rueful appreciation of a joke at his expense.

If Allerton was X, I decided, his crimes had been committed for profit in some way.

It was true that Poirot had not definitely said that X was a man. I considered Miss Cole as a possibility. Her movements were restless and jerky—obviously a woman of nerves. Handsome in a hag-ridden kind of way. Still, she looked normal enough. She, Mrs. Luttrell and Judith were the only women at the dinner table. Mrs. Franklin was having dinner upstairs in her room, and the nurse who attended to her had her meals after us.

After dinner I was standing by the drawing-room window looking out into the garden and thinking back to the time when I had seen Cynthia Murdoch, a young girl with auburn hair, run across

41

that lawn. How charming she had looked in her white overall . . .

Lost in thoughts of the past, I started when Judith passed her arm through mine and impelled me with her out of the window onto the terrace.

She said abruptly, "What's the matter?"

I was startled. "The matter? What do you mean?"

"You've been so queer all through the evening. Why were you staring at everyone at dinner?"

I was annoyed. I had had no idea I had allowed my thoughts so much sway over me.

"Was I? I suppose I was thinking of the past. Seeing ghosts perhaps."

"Oh yes, of course you stayed here, didn't you, when you were a young man? An old lady was murdered here, or something?"

"Poisoned with strychnine."

"What was she like? Nice or nasty?"

I considered the question.

"She was a very kind woman," I said slowly. "Generous. Gave a lot to charity."

"Oh, *that* kind of generosity."

Judith's voice sounded faintly scornful. Then she asked a curious question:

"Were people—happy here?"

No, they had not been happy. That, at least I knew. I said slowly:

"No."

"Why not?"

"Because they felt like prisoners. Mrs. Ingle-

42

thorp, you see, had all the money—and—and doled it out. Her stepchildren could have no life of their own."

I heard Judith take a sharp breath. The hand on my arm tightened.

"That's wicked—wicked. An abuse of power. It shouldn't be allowed. Old people, sick people, they shouldn't have the power to hold up the lives of the young and strong. To keep them tied down, fretting, wasting their power and energy that could be used—that's *needed*. It's just selfishness."

"The old," I said drily, "have not got a monopoly of that quality."

"Oh, I know, Father, you think the young are selfish. So we are, perhaps, but it's a *clean* selfishness. At least we only want to do what we want ourselves, we don't want everybody else to do what we want, we don't want to make slaves of other people."

"No, you just trample them down if they happen to be in your way."

Judith squeezed my arm. She said:

"Don't be so bitter! I don't really do much trampling—and you've never tried to dictate our lives to any of us. We are grateful for that."

"I'm afraid," I said honestly, "that I'd have liked to, though. It was your mother who insisted you should be allowed to make your own mistakes."

Judith gave my arm another quick squeeze. She said:

"I know. You'd have liked to fuss over us like a

hen! I do hate fuss. I won't stand it. But you do agree with me, don't you, about useful lives being sacrificed to useless ones?"

"It does sometimes happen," I admitted. "But there's no need for drastic measures . . . It's up to anybody just to walk out, you know."

"Yes, but is it? *Is* it?"

Her tone was so vehement that I looked at her in some astonishment. It was too dark to see her face clearly. She went on, her voice low and troubled.

"There's so much—it's so difficult—financial considerations, a sense of responsibility, reluctance to hurt someone you've been fond of—all those things, and some people are so unscrupulous— they know just how to play on all those feelings. Some people—some people are like *leeches!*"

"My dear Judith," I exclaimed, taken aback by the positive fury of her tone.

She seemed to realize that she had been over-vehement, for she laughed and withdrew her arm from mine.

"Was I sounding very intense? It's a matter I feel rather hotly about. You see, I've known a case . . . An old brute. And when someone was brave enough to—to cut the knot and set the people she loved free, they called her mad. Mad? It was the sanest thing anyone could do—and the bravest!"

A horrible qualm passed over me. Where, not long ago, had I heard something like that?

"Judith," I said sharply. "Of what case are you talking?"

"Oh, nobody you know. Some friends of the Franklins. Old man called Litchfield. He was quite rich and practically starved his wretched daughters—never let them see anyone, or go out. He was mad, really, but not sufficiently so in the medical sense."

"And the eldest daughter murdered him," I said.

"Oh, I expect you read about it? I suppose you would call it murder—but it wasn't done from personal motives. Margaret Litchfield went straight to the police and gave herself up. I think she was very brave. I wouldn't have had the courage."

"The courage to give yourself up or the courage to commit murder?"

"Both."

"I'm very glad to hear it," I said severely, "and I don't like to hear you talking of murder as justified in certain cases." I paused and added: "What did Dr. Franklin think?"

"Thought it served him right," said Judith. "You know, Father, some people really ask to be murdered."

"I won't have you talking like this, Judith. Who's been putting these ideas into your head?"

"Nobody."

"Well, let me tell you that it's all pernicious nonsense."

"I see. We'll leave it at that." She paused. "I came really to give you a message from Mrs. Franklin.

She'd like to see you if you don't mind coming up to her bedroom."

"I shall be delighted. I'm so sorry she was feeling too ill to come down to dinner."

"She's all right," said Judith unfeelingly. "She just likes making a fuss."

The young are very unsympathetic.

FIVE

I had only met Mrs. Franklin once before. She was a woman about thirty—of what I should describe as the Madonna type. Big brown eyes, hair parted in the centre, and a long gentle face. She was very slender and her skin had a transparent fragility.

She was lying on a day bed, propped up with pillows, and wearing a very dainty negligee of white and pale blue.

Franklin and Boyd Carrington were there drinking coffee. Mrs. Franklin welcomed me with an outstretched hand and a smile.

"How glad I am you've come, Captain Hastings. It will be so nice for Judith. The child has really been working far too hard."

"She looks very well on it," I said as I took the fragile little hand in mine.

Barbara Franklin sighed.

"Yes, she's lucky. How I envy her. I don't believe really that she knows what ill health is. What do you think, Nurse? Oh! Let me introduce you. This is Nurse Craven, who's so terribly, terribly good to me. I don't know what I should do without her. She treats me just like a baby."

Nurse Craven was a tall good-looking young woman with a fine colour and a handsome head of auburn hair. I noticed her hands, which were long and white—very different from the hands of so many hospital nurses. She was in some respects a taciturn girl, and sometimes did not answer. She did not now, merely inclined her head.

"But really," went on Mrs. Franklin, "John has been working that wretched girl of yours too hard. He's such a slave driver. You are a slave driver, aren't you, John?"

Her husband was standing looking out of the window. He was whistling to himself and jingling some loose change in his pocket. He started slightly at his wife's question.

"What's that, Barbara?"

"I was saying that you overwork poor Judith Hastings shamefully. Now Captain Hastings is here, he and I are going to put our heads together and we're not going to allow it."

Persiflage was not Dr. Franklin's strong point.

He looked vaguely worried and turned to Judith inquiringly. He mumbled:

"You must let me know if I overdo it."

Judith said:

"They're just trying to be funny. Talking of work, I wanted to ask you about that stain for the second slide—you know, the one that—"

He turned to her eagerly and broke in.

"Yes, yes. I say, if you don't mind, let's go down to the lab. I'd like to be quite sure—"

Still talking, they went out of the room together.

Barbara Franklin lay back on her pillows. She sighed. Nurse Craven said suddenly and rather disagreeably:

"It's Miss Hastings who's the slave driver, I think!"

Again Mrs. Franklin sighed. She murmured:

"I feel so *inadequate*. I ought, I know, to take more interest in John's work, but I just can't do it. I daresay it's something wrong in me, but—"

She was interrupted by a snort from Boyd Carrington, who was standing by the fireplace.

"Nonsense, Babs," he said. "*You're* all right. Don't worry yourself."

"Oh, but, Bill dear, I *do* worry. I get so discouraged about myself. It's all—I can't help feeling it—it's all so *nasty*. The guinea pigs and the rats and everything. Ugh!" She shuddered. "I know it's stupid, but I'm such a fool. It makes me feel quite sick. I just want to think of all the lovely happy things—birds and flowers, and children playing. *You* know, Bill."

He came over and took the hand she held out to him so pleadingly. His face as he looked down at her was changed, as gentle as any woman's. It was, somehow, impressive—for Boyd Carrington was so essentially a manly man.

"You've not changed much since you were seventeen, Babs," he said. "Do you remember that garden house of yours and the bird bath, and the cocoanuts?"

He turned his head to me.

"Barbara and I are old playmates," he said.

"Oh! Playmates!" she protested.

"Oh, I'm not denying that you're over fifteen years younger than I am. But I played with you as a tiny tot when I was a young man. Gave you pickabacks, my dear. And then later, I came home to find you a beautiful young lady—just on the point of making your debut in the world—and I did my share by taking you out on the golf links and teaching you to play golf. Do you remember?"

"Oh, Bill, do you think I'd forget?"

"My people used to live in this part of the world," she explained to me. "And Bill used to come and stay with his old uncle, Sir Everard, at Knatton."

"And what a mausoleum it was—and is," said Boyd Carrington. "Sometimes I despair of getting the place livable."

"Oh, Bill, it could be made marvellous—quite marvellous!"

"Yes, Babs, but the trouble is I've got no ideas. Baths and some really comfortable chairs—that's all I can think of. It needs a woman."

"I've told you I'll come and help. I mean it. Really."

Sir William looked doubtfully towards Nurse Craven.

"If you're strong enough, I could drive you over. What do you think, Nurse?"

"Oh yes, Sir William. I really think it would do Mrs. Franklin good—if she's careful not to over-tire herself, of course."

"That's a date, then," said Boyd Carrington. "And now you have a good night's sleep. Get into good fettle for tomorrow."

We both wished Mrs. Franklin "Good night" and went out together. As we went down the stairs, Boyd Carrington said gruffly:

"You've no idea what a lovely creature she was at seventeen. I was home from Burma—my wife died out there, you know. Don't mind telling you I completely lost my heart to her. She married Franklin three or four years afterwards. Don't think it's been a happy marriage. It's my idea that that's what lies at the bottom of her ill health. Fellow doesn't understand her or appreciate her. And she's the sensitive kind. I've an idea that this delicacy of hers is partly nervous. Take her out of herself, amuse her, interest her, and she looks a different creature! But that damned sawbones only takes an interest in test tubes and West African natives and cultures."

He snorted angrily.

I thought that there was, perhaps, something in what he said. Yet it surprised me that Boyd Carrington should be attracted by Mrs. Franklin who, when all was said and done, was a sickly creature though pretty in a frail chocolate box way. But Boyd Carrington himself was so full of vitality and life that I should have thought he would merely have been impatient with the neurotic type of invalid. However, Barbara Franklin must have been quite lovely as a girl, and with many men, especially those of the idealistic type such as I judged Boyd Carrington to be, early impressions die hard.

Downstairs Mrs. Luttrell pounced upon us and suggested bridge. I excused myself on the plea of wanting to join Poirot.

I found my friend in bed. Curtiss was moving around the room tidying up, but he presently went out, shutting the door behind him.

"Confound you, Poirot," I said. "You and your infernal habit of keeping things up your sleeve. I've spent the whole evening trying to spot X."

"That must have made you somewhat distrait," observed my friend. "Did nobody comment on your abstraction and ask you what was the matter?"

I reddened slightly, remembering Judith's questions. Poirot, I think, observed my discomfiture. I noticed a small malicious smile on his lips. He merely said, however:

"And what conclusion have you come to on that point?"

"Would you tell me if I was right?"

"Certainly not."

I watched his face closely.

"I had considered Norton—"

Poirot's face did not change.

"Not," I said, "that I've anything to go upon. He just struck me as perhaps less unlikely than anyone else. And then he's—well—inconspicuous. I should imagine the kind of murderer we're after would have to be inconspicuous."

"That is true. But there are more ways than you think of being inconspicuous."

"What do you mean?"

"Supposing, to take a hypothetical case, that if a sinister stranger arrives there some weeks before the murder, for no apparent reason, he will be noticeable. It would be better, would it not, if the stranger were to be a negligible personality, engaged in some harmless sport like fishing?"

"Or watching birds," I agreed. "Yes, but that's just what I was saying."

"On the other hand," said Poirot, "it might be better still if the murderer were already a prominent personality—that is to say, he might be the butcher. That would have the further advantage that no one notices bloodstains on a butcher!"

"You're just being ridiculous. Everyone would know if the butcher had quarrelled with the baker."

"Not if the butcher had become a butcher *simply in order to have a chance of murdering the baker*. One must always look one step behind, my friend."

I looked at him closely, trying to decide if a hint lay concealed in those words. If they meant anything definite, they would seem to point to Colonel Luttrell. Had he deliberately opened a guest house in order to have an opportunity of murdering one of the guests?

Poirot very gently shook his head. He said:

"It is not from my face that you will get the answer."

"You really are a maddening fellow, Poirot," I said with a sigh. "Anyway, Norton isn't my only suspect. What about this fellow Allerton?"

Poirot, his face still impassive, inquired:

"You do not like him?"

"No, I don't."

"Ah. What you call the nasty bit of goods. That is right, is it not?"

"Definitely. Don't you think so?"

"Certainly. He is a man," said Poirot slowly, "very attractive to women."

I made an exclamation of contempt.

"How women can be so foolish. What do they see in a fellow like that?"

"Who can say? But it is always so. The *mauvais sujet*—always women are attracted to him."

"But why?"

Poirot shrugged his shoulders.

"They see something, perhaps, that we do not."

"But what?"

"Danger, possibly . . . Everyone, my friend, demands a spice of danger in their lives. Some get it vicariously—as in bullfights. Some read about it. Some find it at the cinema. But I am sure of this —too much safety is abhorrent to the nature of a human being. Men find danger in many ways— women are reduced to finding their danger mostly in affairs of sex. That is why, perhaps, they welcome the hint of the tiger—the sheathed claws— the treacherous spring. The excellent fellow who will make a good and kind husband—they pass him by."

I considered this gloomily in silence for some minutes. Then I reverted to the previous theme.

"You know, Poirot," I said. "It will be easy enough really for me to find out who X is. I've only got to poke about and find who was acquainted with all the people. I mean the people of your five cases."

I brought this out triumphantly, but Poirot merely gave me a look of scorn.

"I have not demanded your presence here, Hastings, in order to watch you clumsily and laboriously following the way I have already trodden. And let me tell you it is not quite so simple as you think. Four of those cases took place in this county. The people assembled under this roof are not a collection of strangers who have arrived here independently. This is not a hotel in the usual sense of the word. The Luttrells come from this part of the world; they were badly off and bought this place and started it as a venture. The people who come here are their friends, or friends recommended by their friends. Sir William persuaded the Franklins to come. They in turn suggested it to Norton, and, I believe, to Miss Cole—and so on. Which is to say that there is a very fair chance of a certain person who is known to one of these people being known to all of these people. It is also open to X to lure wherever the facts are best known. Take the case of the labourer Riggs. The village where that tragedy occurred is not far from the house of Boyd Carrington's uncle. Mrs. Franklin's people, also, lived near. The inn in the village is much frequented by tourists. Some of Mrs. Franklin's family's friends used to put up there. Franklin himself has stayed there. Norton and Miss Cole may have stayed there and probably have.

"No, no, my friend. I beg that you will not make these clumsy attempts to unravel a secret that I refuse to reveal to you."

"It's so damned silly. As though I should be likely to give it away. I tell you, Poirot, I'm tired of these jokes about my speaking countenance. It's not funny."

Poirot said quietly:

"Are you so sure that is the only reason? Do

you not realize, my friend, that such knowledge may be dangerous? Do you not see that I concern myself with your safety?"

I stared at him open-mouthed. Up till that minute I had not appreciated that aspect of the matter. But it was, of course, true enough. If a clever and resourceful murderer who had already got away with five crimes—unsuspected, as he thought—once awoke to the fact that someone was on his trail, then indeed there was danger for those on his track.

I said sharply:

"But then you—you yourself are in danger, Poirot?"

Poirot, as far as he was able to in his crippled state, made a gesture of supreme disdain.

"I am accustomed to that; I can protect myself. And see, have I not here my faithful dog to protect me also? My excellent and loyal Hastings!"

SIX

Poirot was supposed to keep early hours. I left him therefore to go to sleep and went downstairs, pausing to have a few words with the attendant Curtiss on the way.

I found him a stolid individual, slow in the up-take, but trustworthy and competent. He had been with Poirot since the latter's return from Egypt. His master's health, he told me, was fairly good, but he occasionally had alarming heart attacks, and his heart was much weakened in the last few months. It was a case of the engine slowly failing.

Oh, well, it had been a good life! Nevertheless my heart was wrung for my old friend who was fighting so gallantly every step of the downward way. Even now, crippled and weak, his indomitable spirit was still leading him to ply the craft at which he was so expert.

I went downstairs sad at heart. I could hardly imagine life without Poirot . . .

A rubber was just finishing in the drawing room, and I was invited to cut in. I thought it might serve to distract my mind and I accepted. Boyd Carrington was the one to cut out, and I sat down with Norton and Colonel and Mrs. Luttrell.

"What do you say now, Mr. Norton," said Mrs. Luttrell. "Shall you and I take the other two on? Our late partnership's been very successful."

Norton smiled pleasantly, but murmured "that perhaps, really, they ought to cut—what?"

Mrs. Luttrell assented, but with rather an ill grace, I thought.

Norton and I cut together against the Luttrells. I noticed that Mrs. Luttrell was definitely displeased by this. She bit her lip, and her charm and Irish brogue disappeared completely for the moment.

I soon found out why. I played on many future occasions with Colonel Luttrell, and he was not really such a very bad player. He was what I should describe as a moderate player, but inclined to be forgetful. Every now and then he would make some really bad mistake owing to this. But playing with his wife, he made mistake after mistake without ceasing. He was obviously nervous of her, and this caused him to play about three times as badly as was normal. Mrs. Luttrell herself was a very good player indeed, though a rather unpleasant one to play with. She snatched every conceivable advantage, ignored the rules if her adversary was unaware of them, and enforced them immediately when they served her. She was also extremely adept at a quick sideways glance into her opponent's hand. In other words, she played to win.

And I understood soon enough what Poirot had meant by vinegar. At cards her self-restraint failed, and her tongue lashed every mistake her wretched husband made. It was really most uncomfortable for both Norton and myself, and I was thankful when the rubber came to an end.

We both excused ourselves from playing another on the score of the lateness of the hour.

As we moved away, Norton rather incautiously gave way to his feelings.

"I say, Hastings, that was pretty ghastly. It gets my back up to see that poor old boy bullied like that. And the meek way he takes it! Poor chap. Not much of the peppery-tongued Indian colonel about him."

"Ssh," I warned, for Norton's voice had been raised and I was afraid old Colonel Luttrell would overhear.

"No, but it is too bad."

I said with feeling:

"I shall understand it if he ever takes a hatchet to her."

61

Norton shook his head.

"He won't. The iron's entered into his soul. He'll go on: 'Yes, m'dear, no, m'dear, sorry, m'dear,' pulling at his moustache and bleating meekly until he's put in his coffin. He couldn't assert himself if he tried!"

I shook my head sadly, for I was afraid Norton was right.

We paused in the hall and I noticed that the side door to the garden was open and the wind blowing in.

"Ought we to shut that?" I asked.

Norton hesitated a minute before saying:

"Well—er—I don't think everybody's in yet."

A sudden suspicion darted through my mind. "Who's out?"

"Your daughter, I think—and—er—Allerton."

He tried to make his voice extra casual, but the information coming on top of my conversation with Poirot made me feel suddenly uneasy.

Judith—and Allerton. Surely Judith, my clever, cool Judith, would not be taken in by a man of that type? Surely she would see through him?

I told myself that repeatedly as I undressed, but the vague uneasiness persisted. I could not sleep and lay tossing from side to side.

As is the way with night worries, everything gets exaggerated. A fresh sense of despair and loss swept over me. If only my dear wife were alive. She on whose wise judgment I had relied for so

many years. She had always been wise and understanding about the children.

Without her, I felt miserably inadequate. The
responsibility for their safety and happiness was
mine. Would I be equal to that task? I was not,
Heaven help me, a clever man. I blundered—made
mistakes. If Judith was to ruin her chances of
happiness, if she were to suffer—

Desperately I switched the light on and sat up.

It was no good going on like this. I must get
some sleep. Getting out of bed, I walked over to the
washbasin and looked doubtfully at a bottle of
aspirin tablets.

No, I needed something stronger than aspirin.
I reflected that Poirot, probably, would have some
sleeping stuff of some kind. I crossed the passage
to his room and stood hesitating a minute outside
the door. Rather a shame to wake the old boy up.

As I hesitated, I heard a footfall and looked
round. Allerton was coming along the corridor
towards me. It was dimly lit and until he came
near I could not see his face, and wondered for
a minute who it was. Then I saw, and stiffened
all over. For the man was smiling to himself, and
I disliked that smile very much.

He looked up and raised his eyebrows.

"Hullo, Hastings, still about?"

"I couldn't sleep," I said shortly.

"Is that all? I'll soon fix you up. Come with me."

I followed him into his room, which was the

next one to mine. A strange fascination drove me to study this man as closely as I could.

"You keep late hours yourself," I remarked.

"I've never been an early bed-goer. Not when there's sport abroad. These fine evenings aren't made to be wasted."

He laughed—and I disliked the laugh.

I followed him into the bathroom. He opened a little cupboard and took out a bottle of tablets.

"Here you are. This is the real dope. You'll sleep like a log—and have pleasant dreams, too. Wonderful stuff Slumberyl—that's the patent name for it."

The enthusiasm in his voice gave me a slight shock. Was he a drug taker as well? I said doubtfully:

"It isn't—dangerous?"

"It is if you take too much of it. It's one of the barbiturates—whose toxic dose is very near the effective one." He smiled, the corners of his mouth sliding up his face in an unpleasant way.

"I shouldn't have thought you could get it without a doctor's prescription," I said.

"You can't, old boy. Anyway, quite literally, *you* can't. I've got a pull in that line."

I suppose it was foolish of me, but I get these impulses. I said:

"You knew Etherington, I think?"

At once I knew that I had struck a note of some kind. His eyes grew hard and wary. He said—and his voice had changed—it was light and artificial:

CURTAIN

"Oh yes—I knew Etherington. Poor chap." Then, as I did not speak, he went on: "Etherington took drugs, of course—but he overdid it. One's got to know when to stop. He didn't. Bad business. That wife of his was lucky. If the sympathy of the jury hadn't been with her, she'd have hanged."

He passed me over a couple of the tablets. Then he said casually:

"Did you know Etherington well?"

I answered with the truth.

"No."

He seemed for a moment at a loss how to proceed. Then he turned it off with a light laugh:

"Funny chap. Not exactly a Sunday school character, but he was good company sometimes."

I thanked him for the tablets and went back to my room.

As I lay down again and turned off the lights, I wondered if I had been foolish.

For it came to me very strongly that Allerton was almost certainly X. And I had let him see that I suspected the fact.

SEVEN

My narrative of the days spent at Styles must necessarily be somewhat rambling. In my recollection of it, it presents itself to me as a series of conversations—of suggestive words and phrases that etched themselves into my consciousness.

First of all, and very early on, there came the realization of Hercule Poirot's infirmity and helplessness. I did believe, as he had said, that his brain still functioned with all its old keenness, but the physical envelope had worn so thin that I realized at once that my part was destined to be a far more active one than usual. I had to be, as it were, Poirot's eyes and ears.

True, every fine day Curtiss would pick up his master and carry him carefully downstairs to where his chair had been carried down beforehand and was awaiting him. Then he would wheel Poirot out into the garden and select a spot that was free from draughts. On other days, when the weather was not propitious, he would be carried to the drawing room.

Wherever he might be, someone or other was sure to come and sit with him and talk, but this was not the same thing as if Poirot could have selected for himself his partner in the tête-à-tête. He could no longer single out the person he wanted to talk to.

On the day after my arrival I was taken by Franklin to an old studio in the garden which had been fitted up in a rough-and-ready fashion for scientific purposes.

Let me make clear here and now that I myself have not got the scientific mind. In my account of Dr. Franklin's work I shall probably use all the wrong terms and arouse the scorn of those properly instructed in such matters.

As far as I, a mere layman, could make out, Franklin was experimenting with various alkaloids derived from the Calabar bean, Physostigma venenosum. I understood more after a conversation which took place one day between Franklin and Poirot. Judith, who tried to instruct me, was, as is customary with the earnest young, almost impossibly technical. She referred learnedly to the alkaloids physostigmine, eserine, physovenine, and geneserine, and then proceeded to a most impossible-sounding substance, prostigmin or the demethylcarbonic ester of 3-hydroxyphenyl trimethyl lammonum, etc., etc., and a good deal more which, it appeared, was the same thing, only differently arrived at! It was all, at any rate, double Dutch to me, and I aroused Judith's contempt by asking what good all this was likely to do to mankind? There is no question that annoys your true scientist more. Judith at once threw me a scornful glance and embarked on another lengthy and learned explanation. The upshot of it was, so I gathered, that certain obscure tribes of West African natives had shown a remarkable immunity to an equally obscure, though deadly disease called, as far as I remember, Jordanitis—a certain enthusiastic Dr. Jordan having originally tracked it down. It was an extremely rare tropical ailment, which had been, on one or two occasions, contracted by white people, with fatal results.

I risked inflaming Judith's rage by remarking that it would be more sensible to find some drug that would counteract the aftereffects of measles!

With pity and scorn Judith made it clear to me that it was not the benefaction of the human race, but the enlargement of human knowledge, that was the only goal worthy of attainment.

I looked at some slides through the microscope, studied some photographs of West African natives (really quite entertaining!), caught the eye of a soporific rat in a cage and hurried out again into the air.

As I say, any interest I could feel was kindled by Franklin's conversation with Poirot.

He said:

"You know, Poirot, the stuff's really more up your street than mine. It's the ordeal bean— supposed to prove innocence or guilt. These West African tribes believe it implicitly—or did do so— they're getting sophisticated nowadays. They'll solemnly chew it up quite confident that it will kill them if they're guilty and not harm them if they're innocent."

"And so, alas, they die?"

"No, they don't all die. That's what has always been overlooked up to now. There's a lot behind the whole thing—a medicine man ramp, I rather fancy. There are two distinct species of this bean— only they look so much alike that you can hardly spot the difference. But there *is* a difference. They both contain physostigmine and geneserine and the rest of it, but in the second species you can isolate, or I think I can, yet another alkaloid— and the action of that alkaloid neutralizes the effect of the others. What's more, that second species is regularly eaten by a kind of inner ring in a secret ritual—and the people who eat it never go down with Jordanitis. This third substance has a remarkable effect on the muscular system— without deleterious effects. It's damned interesting. Unfortunately the pure alkaloid is very unstable. Still, I'm getting results. But what's wanted is a lot more research out there on the spot. It's work that ought to be done! Yes, by heck, it is . . . I'd sell my soul to—"

He broke off abruptly. The grin came again.

"Forgive the shop. I get too het up over these things!"

"As you say," said Poirot placidly, "it would certainly make my profession much easier if I could test guilt and innocence so easily. Ah, if there were a substance that could do what is claimed for the Calabar bean!"

Franklin said:

"Ah, but your troubles wouldn't end there! After all, what *is* guilt or innocence?"

"I shouldn't think there could be any doubt about *that*," I remarked.

He turned to me.

"What is evil? What is good? Ideas on them vary from century to century. What you would be testing would probably be a *sense* of guilt or a *sense* of innocence. In fact no value as a test at all."

"I don't see how you make that out."

"My dear fellow, suppose a man thinks he has a divine right to kill a dictator or a moneylender or a pimp or whatever arouses his moral indignation. He commits what *you* consider a guilty deed—but what *he* considers is an innocent one. What is your poor ordeal bean to do about it?"

"Surely," I said, "there must always be a feeling of guilt with murder?"

"Lots of people *I'd* like to kill," said Dr. Franklin

cheerfully. "Don't believe my conscience would keep me awake at night afterwards. It's an idea of mine, you know, that about eighty per cent of the human race ought to be eliminated. We'd get on much better without them."

He got up and strolled away, whistling cheerfully to himself.

I looked after him doubtfully. A low chuckle from Poirot recalled me.

"You look, my friend, like one who has envisaged a nest of serpents. Let us hope that our friend the doctor does not practice what he preaches."

"Ah," I said. "But supposing he does?"

II

After some hesitations I decided that I ought to sound Judith on the subject of Allerton. I felt that I must know what her reactions were. She was, I knew, a level-headed girl, well able to take care of herself, and I did not think that she would really be taken in by the cheap attraction of a man like Allerton. I suppose, actually, that I tackled her on the subject because I wanted to be reassured on that point.

Unfortunately I did not get what I wanted . . . I went about it clumsily, I daresay. There is nothing that young people resent so much as advice from their elders. I tried to make my words quite careless and debonair. I suppose that I failed.

Judith bristled at once.

"What's this?" she said. "A parental warning against the big bad wolf?"

"No, no, Judith, of course not."

"I gather you don't like Major Allerton?"

"Frankly, I don't. Actually I don't suppose you do either."

"Why not?"

"Well—er—he isn't your type, is he?"

"What do you consider is my type, Father?"

Judith can always flurry me. I boggled rather badly. She stood looking at me, her mouth curving upwards in a slightly scornful smile.

"Of course *you* don't like him," she said. "I do. I think he's very amusing."

"Oh, amusing—perhaps." I endeavoured to pass it off.

Judith said deliberately:

"He's very attractive. Any woman would think so. Men, of course, wouldn't see it."

"They certainly wouldn't." I went on, rather clumsily:

"You were out with him very late the other night—"

I was not allowed to finish. The storm broke.

"Really, Father, you're being too idiotic. Don't you realize that at my age I'm capable of managing my own affairs. You've no earthly right to control what I do or whom I choose to make a friend of. It's this senseless interference in their children's lives that is so infuriating about fathers and mothers. I'm very fond of you—but I'm an adult woman and my life is my own. Don't start making a Mr. Barrett of yourself."

I was so hurt by this extremely unkind remark that I was quite incapable of replying and Judith went quickly away.

I was left with the dismayed feeling that I had done more harm than good.

I was standing lost in my thoughts when I was roused by the voice of Mrs. Franklin's nurse exclaiming archly:

"A penny for your thoughts, Captain Hastings!"

I turned gladly to welcome the interruption.

Nurse Craven was really a very good-looking young woman. Her manner was perhaps a little on the arch and sprightly side, but she was pleasant and intelligent.

She had just come from establishing her patient in a sunny spot not far from the improvised laboratory.

"Is Mrs. Franklin interested in her husband's work?" I asked.

Nurse Craven tossed her head contemptuously.

"Oh, it's a good deal too technical for *her*. She's not at all a clever woman, you know, Captain Hastings."

"No, I suppose not."

"Dr. Franklin's work, of course, can only be appreciated by someone who knows something about medicine. He's a very clever man indeed, you know. Brilliant. Poor man, I feel so sorry for him."

"Sorry for him?"

"Yes. I've seen it happen so often. Marrying the wrong type of woman, I mean."

"You think she's the wrong type for him?"

"Well, don't you? They've nothing at all in common."

"He seems very fond of her," I said. "Very attentive to her wishes and all that."

Nurse Craven laughed rather disagreeably.

"She sees to that, all right!"

"You think she trades on her—on her ill health?" I asked doubtfully.

Nurse Craven laughed.

"There isn't much you could teach her about getting her own way. Whatever her ladyship wants happens. Some women are like that—clever as a barrel full of monkeys. If anyone opposes them, they just lie back and shut their eyes and look ill and pathetic, or else they have a nerve storm—but Mrs. Franklin's the pathetic type. Doesn't sleep all night and is all white and exhausted in the morning."

"But she is really an invalid, isn't she?" I asked, rather startled.

Nurse Craven gave me a rather peculiar glance. She said drily:

"Oh, of course," and then turned the subject rather abruptly.

She asked me if it was true that I had been here long ago, in the first war.

"Yes, that's quite true."

She lowered her voice.

"There was a murder here, wasn't there? So one of the maids was telling me. An old lady?"

"Yes."

"And you were there at the time?"

"I was."

She gave a slight shiver. She said:

"That explains it, doesn't it?"

"Explains what?"

She gave me a quick sideways glance.

"The—the atmosphere of the place. Don't· you feel it? I do. Something *wrong*, if you know what I mean?"

I was silent a moment considering. Was it true what she had just said? Did the fact that death by violence—by malice aforethought—had taken place in a certain spot leave its impression on that spot so strongly that it was perceptible after many years? Psychic people said so. Did Styles definitely bear traces of that event that had occurred so long ago? Here, within these walls, in these gardens, thoughts of murder had lingered and grown stronger and had at last come to fruition in the final act. Did they still taint the air?

Nurse Craven broke in on my thoughts by saying abruptly:

"I was in a house where there was a murder case once. I've never forgotten it. One doesn't,

76

you know. One of my patients. I had to give evidence and everything. Made me feel quite queer. It's a nasty experience for a girl."

"It must be. I know myself—"

I broke off as Boyd Carrington came striding round the corner of the house.

As usual, his big buoyant personality seemed to sweep away shadows and intangible worries. He was so large, so sane, so out of doors—one of those lovable, forceful personalities that radiate cheerfulness and common sense.

"Morning, Hastings; morning, Nurse. Where's Mrs. Franklin?"

"Good morning, Sir William. Mrs. Franklin's down at the bottom of the garden under the beech tree near the laboratory."

"And Franklin, I suppose, is *inside* the laboratory?"

"Yes, Sir William—with Miss Hastings."

"Wretched girl. Fancy being cooped up doing stinks on a morning like this! You ought to protest, Hastings."

Nurse Craven said quickly:

"Oh, Miss Hastings is *quite* happy. She likes it, you know, and the doctor couldn't do without her, I'm sure."

"Miserable fellow," said Boyd Carrington. "If I had a pretty girl like your Judith as a secretary, I'd be looking at *her* instead of at guinea pigs, eh what?"

It was the kind of joke that Judith would particularly have disliked, but it went down quite well with Nurse Craven, who laughed a good deal.

"Oh, Sir William," she exclaimed. "You really mustn't say things like that. I'm sure we all know what *you'd* be like! But poor Dr. Franklin is so serious—quite wrapped up in his work."

Boyd Carrington said cheerfully:

"Well, his wife seems to have taken up her position where she can keep her eye on her husband. I believe she's jealous."

"You know far too much, Sir William!"

Nurse Craven seemed delighted with this badinage. She said reluctantly:

"Well, I suppose I ought to be going to see about Mrs. Franklin's malted milk."

She moved away slowly and Boyd Carrington stood looking after her.

"Good-looking girl," he remarked. "Lovely hair and teeth. Fine specimen of womanhood. Must be a dull life on the whole always looking after sick people. A girl like that deserves a better fate."

"Oh, well," I said. "I suppose she'll marry one day."

"I expect so."

He sighed—and it occurred to me that he was thinking of his dead wife. Then he said:

"Like to come over with me to Knatton and see the place?"

"Rather. I'd like to. I'll just see first if Poirot needs me."

I found Poirot sitting on the verandah, well muffled up. He encouraged me to go.

"But certainly go, Hastings, go. It is, I believe, a most handsome property. You should certainly see it."

"I'd like to. But I didn't want to desert you."

"My faithful friend! No, no, go with Sir William. A charming man, is he not?"

"First class," I said with enthusiasm.

Poirot smiled.

"Ah yes. I thought he was your type."

III

I enjoyed my expedition enormously.

Not only was the weather fine—a really lovely summer's day—but I enjoyed the companionship of the man.

Boyd Carrington had that personal magnetism, that wide experience of life and of places that made him excellent company. He told me stories of his administrative days in India, some intriguing details of East African tribal lore and was altogether so interesting that I was quite taken out of myself and forgot my worries about Judith and the deep anxieties that Poirot's revelations had given me.

I liked, too, the way Boyd Carrington spoke of my friend. He had a deep respect for him—both for his work and his character. Sad though Poirot's present condition of ill health was, Boyd Carrington uttered no facile words of pity. He seemed to think that a lifetime spent as Poirot's had been was in itself a rich reward and that in his memories my friend could find satisfaction and self-respect.

"Moreover," he said, "I'd wager his brain is as keen as ever it was."

"It is; indeed it is," I assented eagerly.

"No greater mistake than to think that because a man's tied by the leg it affects his brain pan. Not a bit of it. Anno Domini affects headwork much less than you'd think. By Jove, I wouldn't care to undertake to commit a murder under Hercule Poirot's nose—even at this time of day."

"He'd get you if you did," I said, grinning.

"I bet he would. Not," he added ruefully, "that I should be much good at doing a murder anyway. I can't plan things, you know. Too impatient. If I did a murder, it would be done on the spur of the moment."

"That might be the most difficult crime to spot."

"I hardly think so. I'd probably leave clues trailing along behind me in every direction. Well, it's lucky I haven't got a criminal mind. Only kind of man I can imagine myself killing is a blackmailer. That is a foul thing, if you like. I've always thought a blackmailer ought to be shot. What do you say?"

I confessed to some sympathy with his point of view.

Then we passed on to an examination of the

work done on the house as a young architect came forward to meet us.

Knatton was mainly of Tudor date with a wing added later. It had not been modernized or altered since the installation of two primitive bathrooms in the eighteen-forties or thereabouts.

Boyd Carrington explained that his uncle had been more or less of a hermit, disliking people and living in a corner of the vast house. Boyd Carrington and his brother had been tolerated, and had spent their holidays there as schoolboys before Sir Everard had become as much of a recluse as he afterwards became.

The old man had never married, and had spent only a tenth of his large income, so that even after death duties had been paid, the present baronet had found himself a very rich man.

"But a very lonely one," he said, sighing.

I was silent. My sympathy was too acute to be put into words. For I, too, was a lonely man. Since Cinders had died, I felt myself to be only half a human being.

Presently, a little haltingly, I expressed a little of what I felt.

"Ah yes, Hastings, but you've had something I never had."

He paused a moment and then—rather jerkily he gave me an outline of his own tragedy.

Of the beautiful young wife, a lovely creature full of charm and accomplishments but with a tainted heritage. Her family had nearly all died of drink, and she herself fell a victim to the same curse. Barely a year after their marriage she had succumbed and had died a dipsomaniac's death. He did not blame her. He realized that heredity had been too strong for her.

After her death he had settled down to lead a lonely life. He had determined, saddened by his experience, not to marry again.

"One feels," he said simply, "safer alone."

"Yes, I can understand your feeling like that— at any rate at first."

"The whole thing was such a tragedy. It left me prematurely aged and embittered." He paused. "It's true—I was once very much tempted. But she was so young—I didn't feel it would be fair to tie her to a disillusioned man. I was too old for her— she was such a child—so pretty—so completely untouched."

He broke off, shaking his head.

"Wasn't that for her to judge?"

"I don't know, Hastings. I thought not. She— she seemed to like me. But then, as I say, she was so young. I shall always remember her as I saw her the last day of that leave. Her head a little on one side—that slightly bewildered look—her little hand—"

He stopped. The words conjured up a picture that seemed vaguely familiar, though I could not think why.

Boyd Carrington's voice, suddenly harsh, broke into my thoughts.

"I was a fool," he said. "Any man is a fool who lets opportunity slip by him. Anyway, here I am, with a great mansion of a house far too big for me, and no gracious presence to sit at the head of my table."

To me there was a charm in his slightly old-fashioned way of putting things. It conjured up a picture of old-world charm and ease.

"Where is the lady now?" I asked.

"Oh—married." He turned it off briefly. "Fact is, Hastings, I'm cut out now for a bachelor existence. I've got my little ways. Come and look at the gardens. They've been badly neglected, but they're very fine in their way."

We walked round the place and I was much impressed with all I saw. Knatton was undoubtedly a very fine estate and I did not wonder that Boyd Carrington was proud of it. He knew the neighbourhood well and most of the people roundabout, though of course there had been newcomers since his time.

He had known Colonel Luttrell in the old days and expressed his earnest hope that the Styles venture was going to pay.

"Poor old Toby Luttrell's very hard up, you know," he said. "Nice fellow. Good soldier, too, and a very fine shot. Went on safari with him in Africa once. Ah, those were the days! He was married then, of course, but his missus didn't come along, thank goodness. Pretty woman she was—but always a bit of a Tartar. Funny the things a man will stand from a woman. Old Toby Luttrell who used to make subalterns shake in their shoes, he was such a stern martinet! And there he is, henpecked and bullied and meek as they make 'em! No doubt about it, that woman's got a tongue like vinegar. Still, she's got a head on her. If anyone can make the place pay, she will. Luttrell never had much of a head for business—but Mrs. Toby would skin her grandmother!"

"She's so gushing with it all," I complained.

Boyd Carrington looked amused.

"I know. All sweetness. But have you played bridge with them?"

I replied feelingly that I had.

"On the whole I steer clear of women bridge players," said Boyd Carrington. "And if you take my tip, you'll do the same."

I told him how uncomfortable Norton and myself had felt on the first evening of my arrival.

"Exactly. One doesn't know where to look!"

He added:

"Nice fellow, Norton. Very quiet though. Always looking at birds and things. Doesn't care for shooting them, he told me. Extraordinary! No feeling for sport. I told him he missed a lot. Can't see myself what excitement there can be stalking about through cold woods peering at birds through glasses."

How little we realized then that Norton's hobby might have an important part to play in the events that were to come.

EIGHT

The days passed. It was an unsatisfactory time
—with its uneasy feeling of waiting for something.

Nothing, if I may put it in such a way, actually
happened. Yet there were incidents, scraps of odd
conversations, sidelights upon the various inmates
of Styles, elucidating remarks. They all mounted
up and, if properly pieced together, could have
done a lot towards enlightening me.

It was Poirot who, with a few forceful words,
showed me something to which I had been crimi-
nally blind.

I was complaining, for the umpteenth time, of
his wilful refusal to admit me to his confidence.
It was not fair, I told him. Always he and I had
had equal knowledge—even if I had been dense

85

and he had been astute in drawing the right conclusions from that knowledge.

He waved an impatient hand.

"Quite so, my friend. It is not fair! It is not sporting! It is not playing the game! Admit all that and pass from it. This is *not* a game—it is not *le sport*. For you, you occupy yourself in guessing wildly at the identity of X. It is not for that that I asked you to come here. Unnecessary for you to occupy yourself with that. *I* know the answer to that question. But what I do not know and what I must know is this: 'Who is going to die—very soon?' It is a question, *mon vieux*, not of you playing a guessing game, but of preventing a human being from dying."

I was startled.

"Of course," I said slowly. "I—well, I did know that you practically said so once, but I haven't quite realized it."

"Then realize it now—immediately."

"Yes, yes, I will—I mean, I do."

"*Bien!* Then tell me, Hastings, who is it who is going to die?"

I stared at him blankly.

"I have really no idea!"

"Then you should have an idea! What else are you here for?"

"Surely," I said, going back over my meditations on the subject, "there must be a connection between the victim and X so that if you told me who X was—"

Poirot shook his head with so much vigour that it was quite painful to watch.

"Have I not told you that that is the essence of X's technique? There will be nothing connecting X with the death. That is certain."

"The connection will be hidden, you mean?"

"It will be so well hidden that neither you nor I will find it."

"But surely by studying X's past—"

"I tell you, no. Certainly not in the *time*. Murder may happen any moment, you comprehend?"

"To someone in this house?"

"To someone in this house."

"And you really do not know who, or how?"

"Ah, if I did, I should not be urging you to find out for me!"

"You simply base your assumption on the presence of X?"

I sounded a little doubtful. Poirot, whose self-control had lessened as his limbs were perforce immobile, fairly howled at me.

"Ah, *ma foi*, how many times am I to go over all this? If a lot of war correspondents arrive suddenly in a certain spot of Europe, it means what? It means war! If doctors come from all over the world to a certain city—it shows what? That there is to be a medical conference. Where you see a vulture hovering, there will be a carcass. If you see beaters walking up a moor, there will be a shoot. If you see a man stop suddenly, tear off his coat and plunge into the sea, it means that there, there will be a rescue from drowning.

"If you see ladies of middle age and respectable appearance peering through a hedge, you may deduce that there is an impropriety of some kind! And finally, if you smell a succulent smell and observe several people all walking along a corridor in the same direction, you may safely assume that a meal is about to be served!"

I considered these analogies for a minute or two, then I said, taking the first one:

"All the same, one war correspondent does not make a war!"

"Certainly not. And one swallow does not make a summer. But one murderer, Hastings, does make a murder."

That, of course, was undeniable. But it still occurred to me, as it did not seem to have occurred to Poirot, that even a murderer has his off times. X might be at Styles simply for a holiday with no lethal intent. Poirot was so worked up, however, that I dared not propound this suggestion. I merely said that the whole thing seemed to me hopeless. We must wait—

"And see," finished Poirot. "Like your Mr. Asquith in the last war. That, *mon cher*, is just what we must not do. I do not say, mark you, that we shall succeed, for as I have told you before, when a killer has determined to kill, it is not easy to circumvent him. But we can at least try. Figure to yourself, Hastings, that you have here the bridge problem in the paper. You can see all the cards. What you are asked to do is 'Forecast the result of the deal.' "

I shook my head.

"It's no good, Poirot. I haven't the least idea. If I knew who X was—"

Poirot howled at me again. He howled so loud that Curtiss came running in from the next room looking quite frightened. Poirot waved him away and when he had gone out again, my friend spoke in a more controlled manner.

"Come, Hastings, you are not so stupid as you like to pretend. You have studied those cases I gave you to read. You may not know who X is, but you know X's technique for committing a crime."

"Oh," I said. "I see."

"Of course you see. The trouble with you is that you are mentally lazy. You like to play games and guess. You do not like to work with your head. What is the essential element of X's technique? Is it not that the crime, when committed, is complete? That is to say, there is a motive for the crime, there is an opportunity, there is means and there is, last and most important, the guilty person all ready for the dock."

At once I grasped the essential point and realized what a fool I had been not to see it sooner.

"I see," I said. "I've got to look round for somebody who—who answers to those requirements—the potential victim."

Poirot leaned back with a sigh.

"*Enfin!* I am very tired. Send Curtiss to me. You understand your job now. You are active, you can get about, you can follow people about, talk to them, spy upon them unobserved—" (I nearly uttered an indignant protest, but quelled it. It was too old an argument.) "You can listen to conversations, you have knees that will still bend and permit you to kneel and look through keyholes—"

"I will not look through keyholes," I interrupted hotly.

Poirot closed his eyes.

"Very well, then. You will not look through keyholes. You will remain the English gentleman and someone will be killed. It does not matter, that. Honour comes first with an Englishman. Your honour is more important than somebody else's life. *Bien!* It is understood."

"No, but dash it all, Poirot—"

Poirot said coldly:

"Send Curtiss to me. Go away. You are obstinate and extremely stupid and I wish that there were someone else whom I could trust, but I suppose I shall have to put up with you and your absurd ideas of fair play. Since you cannot use your grey cells as you do not possess them, at any rate use your eyes, your ears and your nose if need be in so far as the dictates of honour allow."

II

It was on the following day that I ventured to broach an idea which had come into my mind more than once. I did so a little dubiously, for one never knows how Poirot may react!

I said:

"I've been thinking, Poirot. I know I'm not much of a fellow. You've said I'm stupid. Well, in a way it's true. And I'm only half the man I was. Since Cinders' death—"

I stopped. Poirot made a gruff noise indicative of sympathy.

I went on:

"But there is a man here who could help us—just the kind of man we need. Brains, imagination, resource—used to making decisions and a man of wide experience. I'm talking of Boyd Carrington. He's the man we want, Poirot. Take him into your confidence. Put the whole thing before him."

Poirot opened his eyes and said with immense decision:

"Certainly not."

"But why not? You can't deny that he's clever—a good deal cleverer than I am."

"That," said Poirot with biting sarcasm, "would be easy. But dismiss the idea from your mind, Hastings. We take *no one* into our confidence. That is understood—*hein*? You comprehend, I forbid you to speak of this matter."

"All right, if you say so, but really Boyd Carrington—"

"Ah ta ta! Boyd Carrington. Why are you so obsessed with Boyd Carrington? What is he, after all? A big man who is pompous and pleased with himself because people have called him 'Your Excellency.' A man with—yes, a certain amount of tact and charm of manner. But he is not so wonderful, your Boyd Carrington. He repeats himself, he tells the same story twice—and what is more, his memory is so bad that he tells back to you the story that you have told to him! A man of outstanding ability? Not at all. An old bore—a windbag—*enfin*—the stuffed shirt!"

"Oh," I said as enlightenment came to me.

It was quite true that Boyd Carrington's memory was not good. And he had actually been guilty of a *gaffe* which I now saw had annoyed Poirot a good deal. Poirot had told him a story of his police days in Belgium, and only a couple of days afterwards, when several of us were assembled in the garden, Boyd Carrington had in bland forgetfulness told the same story back again to Poirot, prefacing it with the remark: "I remember the Chef de la Sûreté in Paris telling me—"

I now perceived that this had rankled!

Tactfully, I said no more and withdrew.

CURTAIN

III

I wandered downstairs and out into the garden. There was no one about and I strolled through a grove of trees and up to a grassy knoll which was surmounted by a somewhat earwiggy summer-house in an advanced stage of decrepitude. Here I sat down, lit my pipe, and settled down to think things out.

Who was there at Styles who had a fairly definite motive for murdering somebody else—or who might be made out to have one?

Putting aside the somewhat obvious case of Colonel Luttrell who, I was afraid, was hardly likely to take a hatchet to his wife in the middle of a rubber, justifiable though that course might be, I could not at first think of anyone.

The trouble was that I did not really know enough about these people. Norton, for instance, and Miss Cole? What were the usual motives for murder? Money? Boyd Carrington was, I fancied, the only rich man of the party. If he died, who would inherit that money? Anyone at present in the house? I hardly thought so, but it was a point that might bear inquiry. He might, for instance, have left his money to research, making Franklin a trustee. That, with the doctor's rather injudicious remarks on the subject of eliminating 80 per cent of the human race, might make out a fairly damning case against the red-haired doctor. Or possibly

Norton or Miss Cole might be a distant relative and would inherit automatically. Far-fetched but possible. Would Colonel Luttrell, who was an old friend, benefit under Boyd Carrington's will? These possibilities seemed to exhaust the money angle. I turned to more romantic possibilities. The Franklins. Mrs. Franklin was an invalid. Was it possible that she was being slowly poisoned—and would the responsibility for her death be laid at her husband's door? He was a doctor; he had opportunity and means, no doubt. What about motive? An unpleasant qualm shot across my mind as it occurred to me that Judith might be involved. I had good reason to know how businesslike their relations were—but would the general public believe that? Would a cynical police officer believe it? Judith was a very beautiful young woman. An attractive secretary or assistant had been the motive for many crimes. The possibility dismayed me.

I considered Allerton next. Could there be any reason for doing away with Allerton? If we had to have a murder, I would prefer to see Allerton the victim! One ought to be able to find motives easily for doing away with him. Miss Cole, though not young, was still a good-looking woman. She might, conceivably, be actuated by jealousy if she and Allerton had ever been on intimate terms, though I had no reason to believe that that was the case. Besides, if Allerton was X—

I shook my head impatiently. All this was getting me nowhere. A footstep on the gravel below attracted my attention. It was Franklin walking rapidly towards the house, his hands in his pockets, his head thrust forward. His whole attitude was one of dejection. Seeing him thus, off guard, I was struck by the fact that he looked a thoroughly unhappy man.

I was so busy staring at him that I did not hear a footfall nearer at hand and turned with a start when Miss Cole spoke to me.

"I didn't hear you coming," I explained apologetically as I sprang up.

She was examining the summerhouse.

"What a Victorian relic!"

"Isn't it? It's rather spidery, I'm afraid. Do sit down. I'll dust the seat for you."

For it occurred to me that here was a chance to get to know one of my fellow guests a little better. I studied Miss Cole covertly as I brushed away cobwebs.

She was a woman of between thirty and forty, slightly haggard, with a clear-cut profile and really very beautiful eyes. There was about her an air of reserve, more—of suspicion. It came to me suddenly that this was a woman who had suffered and who was, in consequence, deeply distrustful of life. I felt that I would like to know more about Elizabeth Cole.

"There," I said with a final flick of the handkerchief, "that's the best I can do."

"Thank you." She smiled and sat down. I sat

down beside her. The seat creaked ominously, but no catastrophe occurred.

Miss Cole said:

"Do tell me, what were you thinking about when I came up to you? You seemed quite sunk in thought."

I said slowly:

"I was watching Dr. Franklin."

"Yes?"

I saw no reason for not repeating what had been in my mind.

"It struck me that he looked a very unhappy man."

The woman beside me said quietly:

"But of course he is. You must have realized that."

I think I showed my surprise. I said, stammering slightly:

"No—no—I haven't. I've always thought of him as absolutely wrapped up in his work."

"So he is."

"Do you call that unhappiness? I should have said it was the happiest state imaginable."

"Oh yes, I'm not disputing it—but not if you're hampered from doing what you feel it's in you to do. If you can't, that is to say, produce your best."

I looked at her, feeling rather puzzled. She went on to explain.

"Last autumn, Dr. Franklin was offered the chance of going out to Africa and continuing his research work there. He's tremendously keen, as you know, and has really done first-class work already in the realm of tropical medicine."

"And he didn't go?"

"No. His wife protested. She herself wasn't well enough to stand the climate and she kicked against the idea of being left behind, especially as it would have meant very economical living for her. The pay offered was not high."

"Oh," I said. I went on slowly: "I suppose he felt that in her state of health he couldn't leave her."

"Do you know much about her state of health, Captain Hastings?"

"Well, I—no— But she is an invalid, isn't she?"

"She certainly enjoys bad health," said Miss Cole drily. I looked at her doubtfully. It was easy to see that her sympathies were entirely with the husband.

"I suppose," I said slowly, "that women who are —delicate are apt to be selfish?"

"Yes, I think invalids—chronic invalids—usually are very selfish. One can't blame them perhaps. It's so easy."

"You don't think that there's really very much the matter with Mrs. Franklin?"

"Oh, I shouldn't like to say that. It's just a suspicion. She always seems able to do anything she wants to do."

I reflected in silence for a minute or two. It struck me that Miss Cole seemed very well acquainted with the ramifications of the Franklin ménage. I asked with some curiosity:

"You know Dr. Franklin well, I suppose?"

She shook her head.

"Oh no. I had only met them once or twice before we met here."

"But he has talked to you about himself, I suppose?"

Again she shook her head.

"No, what I have just told you I learnt from your daughter Judith."

Judith, I reflected with a moment's bitterness, talked to everyone except me.

Miss Cole went on:

"Judith is terrifically loyal to her employer and very much up in arms on his behalf. Her condemnation of Mrs. Franklin's selfishness is sweeping."

"You, too, think she is selfish?"

"Yes, but I can see her point of view. I—I—understand invalids. I can understand, too, Dr. Franklin's giving way to her. Judith, of course, thinks he should park his wife anywhere and get on with the job. Your daughter's a very enthusiastic scientific worker."

"I know," I said rather disconsolately. "It worries me sometimes. It doesn't seem natural, if you know what I mean. I feel she ought to be—more human—more keen on having a good time. Amuse herself—fall in love with a nice boy or two. After all, youth is the time to have one's fling—not to sit poring over test tubes. It isn't natural. In our young days we were having fun—flirting—enjoying ourselves—*you* know."

There was a moment's silence. Then Miss Cole said in a queer cold voice:

"I don't know."

I was instantly horrified. Unconsciously I had spoken as though she and I were contemporaries —but I realized suddenly that she was well over ten years my junior and that I had been unwittingly extremely tactless.

I apologized as best I could. She cut into my stammering phrases.

"No, no, I didn't mean that. Please don't apologize. I meant just simply what I said. *I don't know.* I was never what you mean by 'young.' I never had what is called 'a good time.'"

Something in her voice, a bitterness, a deep resentment, left me at a loss. I said rather lamely but with sincerity:

"I'm sorry."

She smiled.

"Oh, well, it doesn't matter. Don't look so upset. Let's talk about something else."

I obeyed.

"Tell me something about the other people here," I said. "Unless they're all strangers to you."

"I've known the Luttrells all my life. It's rather sad that they should have to do this—especially for him. He's rather a dear. And she's nicer than you'd think. It's having had to pinch and scrape all her life that has made her rather—well—predatory. If you're always on the make, it does tell in the end. The only thing I do rather dislike about her is that gushing manner."

"Tell me something about Mr. Norton."

"There isn't really much to tell. He's very nice —rather shy—just a little stupid, perhaps. He's always been rather delicate. He's lived with his mother—rather a peevish, stupid woman. She bossed him a good deal, I think. She died a few years ago. He's keen on birds and flowers and things like that. He's a very kind person—and he's the sort of person who sees a lot."

"Through his glasses, you mean?"

Miss Cole smiled.

"Well, I wasn't meaning it quite so literally as that. I meant more that he *notices* a good deal. Those quiet people often do. He's unselfish—and very considerate for a man, but he's rather—ineffectual, if you know what I mean."

I nodded.

"Oh yes, I know."

Elizabeth Cole said suddenly, and once more the deep bitter note was in her voice:

"That's the depressing part of places like this. Guest houses run by broken-down gentlepeople. They're full of failures—of people who have never got anywhere and never will get anywhere, of people who—who have been defeated and broken by life, of people who are old and tired and finished."

Her voice died away. A deep and spreading sadness permeated me. How true it was! Here we were, a collection of twilit people. *Grey heads, grey hearts, grey dreams.* Myself, sad and lonely, the woman beside me also a bitter and disillusioned creature. Dr. Franklin, his ambitions curbed and thwarted, his wife a prey to ill health. Quiet little Norton limping about looking at birds. Even Poirot, the once brilliant Poirot, now a broken, crippled old man.

How different it had been in the old days—the days when I had first come to Styles. The thought was too much for me—a stifled exclamation of pain and regret came to my lips.

My companion said quickly:

"What is it?"

"Nothing. I was just struck by the contrast—I was here, you know, many years ago, as a young man. I was thinking of the difference between then and now."

"I see. It was a happy house then? Everyone was happy here?"

Curious, sometimes, how one's thoughts seemed to swing in a kaleidoscope. It happened to me now. A bewildering shuffling and reshuffling of memories, of events. Then the mosaic settled into its true pattern.

My regret had been for the past as the past, not for the reality. For even then, in that far-off time, there had been no happiness at Styles. I remembered dispassionately the real facts. My friend John and his wife, both unhappy and chafing at the life they were forced to lead. Lawrence Cavendish, sunk in melancholy. Cynthia, her girlish brightness dampened by her dependent position. Inglethorp married to a rich woman for her money. No, none of them had been happy. And now, again, no one here was happy. Styles was not a lucky house.

I said to Miss Cole:

"I've been indulging in false sentiment. This was never a happy house. It isn't now. Everyone here is unhappy."

"No, no. Your daughter—"

"Judith's not happy."

I said it with the certainty of sudden knowledge. No, Judith wasn't happy.

"Boyd Carrington," I said doubtfully. "He was saying the other day that he was lonely—but for all that I think he's enjoying himself quite a good deal—what with his house and one thing and another."

Miss Cole said sharply:

"Oh yes, but then Sir William is different. He doesn't belong here like the rest of us do. He's from the outside world—the world of success and independence. He's made a success of his life and he knows it. He's not one of—of the maimed."

It was a curious word to choose. I turned and stared at her.

"Will you tell me," I asked, "why you used that particular expression?"

"Because," she said with a sudden fierce energy,

"it's the truth. The truth about me, at any rate. I am maimed."

"I can see," I said gently, "that you have been very unhappy."

She said quietly:

"You don't know who I am, do you?"

"Er—I know your name—"

"Cole isn't my name—that is to say, it was my mother's name. I took it—afterwards."

"After?"

"My real name is Litchfield."

For a minute or two it didn't sink in—it was just a name vaguely familiar. Then I remembered.

"Matthew Litchfield."

She nodded.

"I see you know about it. That was what I meant just now. My father was an invalid and a tyrant. He forbade us any kind of normal life. We couldn't ask friends to the house. He kept us short of money. We were—in prison."

She paused, her eyes, those beautiful eyes, wide and dark.

"And then my sister—my sister—"

She stopped.

"Please don't—don't go on. It is too painful for you. I know about it. There is no need to tell me."

"But you don't know. You can't. Maggie. It's inconceivable—unbelievable. I know that she went to the police, that she gave herself up, that she confessed. But I still sometimes can't believe it! I feel somehow that it wasn't true—that it didn't—that it couldn't have happened like she said it did."

"You mean"—I hesitated—"that the facts were at—at variance—"

She cut me short.

"No, no. Not that. No, it's Maggie herself. It wasn't *like* her. It wasn't—it wasn't *Maggie!*"

Words trembled on my lips, but I did not say them. The time had not yet come when I could say to her:

"You are right. *It wasn't Maggie . . .*"

NINE

It must have been about six o'clock when Colonel Luttrell came along the path. He had a rook rifle with him and was carrying a couple of dead wood pigeons.

He started when I hailed him and seemed surprised to see us.

"Hullo, what are you two doing there? That tumbledown old place isn't very safe, you know. It's falling to pieces. Probably break up about your ears. Afraid you'll get dirty there, Elizabeth."

"Oh, that's all right. Captain Hastings has sacrificed a pocket handkerchief in the good cause of keeping my dress clean."

The Colonel murmured vaguely:

"Oh, really? Oh well, that's all right."

He stood there pulling at his lip and we got up and joined him.

His mind seemed far away this evening. He roused himself to say:

"Been trying to get some of these cursed wood pigeons. Do a lot of damage, you know."

"You're a very fine shot, I hear," I told him.

"Eh? Who told you that? Oh, Boyd Carrington. Used to be—used to be. Bit rusty nowadays. Age will tell."

"Eyesight," I suggested.

He negatived the suggestion immediately.

"Nonsense. Eyesight's as good as ever it was. That is—have to wear glasses for reading, of course. But far sight's all right."

He repeated a minute or two later:

"Yes—all right. Not that it matters . . ."

His voice tailed off into an absent-minded mutter.

Miss Cole said, looking round:

"What a beautiful evening it is."

She was quite right. The sun was drawing to the west and the light was a rich golden, bringing out the deeper shades of green in the trees in a deep, glowing effect. It was an evening, still and calm, and very English, such as one remembers when in far-off tropical countries. I said as much.

Colonel Luttrell agreed eagerly.

"Yes, yes, often used to think of evenings like this—out in India, you know. Makes you look forward to retiring and settling down—what?"

I nodded. He went on, his voice changing:

"Yes, settling down—coming home—nothing's ever quite what you picture it—no—no."

I thought that that was probably particularly true in his case. He had not pictured himself running a guest house, trying to make it pay, with a nagging wife forever snapping at him and complaining.

We walked slowly towards the house. Norton and Boyd Carrington were sitting on the verandah and the Colonel and I joined them while Miss Cole went on into the house.

We chatted for a few minutes. Colonel Luttrell seemed to have brightened up. He made a joke or two and seemed far more cheerful and wide-awake than usual.

"Been a hot day," said Norton. "I'm thirsty."

"Have a drink, you fellows. On the house, what?" The Colonel sounded eager and happy.

We thanked him and accepted. He got up and went in.

The part of the terrace where we were sitting was just outside the dining-room window, and that window was open.

We heard the Colonel inside—opening a cupboard, then heard the squeak of a corkscrew and the subdued pop as the cork of the bottle came out.

And then, sharp and high came the unofficial voice of Mrs. Colonel Luttrell!

"What are you doing, George?"

The Colonel's voice was subdued to a mutter.

We only heard a mumbled word here and there—
fellows outside—drink—

The sharp, irritating voice burst out indignantly:

"You'll do no such thing, George. The idea now.
How do you think we'll ever make this place pay if
you go round standing everybody drinks? Drinks
here will be paid for. *I've* got a business head if
you haven't. Why, you'd be bankrupt tomorrow if
it wasn't for me! I've got to look after you like a
child. Yes, just like a child. You've got no sense at
all. Give me that bottle. Give it me, I say."

Again there was an agonized low protesting
mumble.

Mrs. Luttrell answered snappishly:

"I don't care whether they do or they don't. The
bottle's going back in the cupboard, and I'm going
to lock the cupboard too."

There was the sound of a key being turned in
the lock.

"There now. That's the way of it."

This time the Colonel's voice came more clearly:

"You're going too far, Daisy. I won't have it."

"*You* won't have it? And who are you, I'd like
to know? Who runs this house? I do. And don't
you forget it."

There was a faint swish of draperies and Mrs.
Luttrell evidently flounced out of the room.

It was some few moments before the Colonel
reappeared. He looked in those few moments to
have grown much older and feebler.

There was not one of us who did not feel deeply

sorry for him and who would not willingly have murdered Mrs. Luttrell.

"Awfully sorry, you chaps," he said, his voice sounding stiff and unnatural. "Seem to have run out of whisky."

He must have realized that we could not have helped overhearing what had passed. If he had not realized it, our manner would soon have told him. We were all miserably uncomfortable, and Norton quite lost his head, hurriedly saying first that he didn't really want a drink—too near dinner, wasn't it, and then elaborately changing the subject and making a series of the most unconnected remarks. It was indeed a bad moment. I myself felt paralyzed and Boyd Carrington, who was the only one of us who might conceivably have managed to pass it off, got no opportunity with Norton's babble.

Out of the tail of my eye I saw Mrs. Luttrell stalking away down one of the paths equipped with gardening gloves and a dandelion weeder. She was certainly an efficient woman, but I felt bitterly towards her just then. No human being has a right to humiliate another human being.

Norton was still talking feverishly. He had picked up a wood pigeon and from first telling us how he had been laughed at at his prep school for being sick when he saw a rabbit killed, had gone on to the subject of grouse moors, telling a long and rather pointless story of an accident that had occurred in Scotland when a beater had been shot. We talked of various shooting accidents we had known, and then Boyd Carrington cleared his throat and said:

"Rather an amusing thing happened once with a batman of mine. Irish chap. He had a holiday and went off to Ireland for it. When he came back, I asked him if he had had a good holiday.

"'Ah shure, your Honour, best holiday I've ever had in my life!'

"'I'm glad of that,' I said, rather surprised at his enthusiasm.

"'Ah yes, shure, it was a grand holiday! I shot my brother.'

"'You shot your brother!' I exclaimed.

"'Ah yes, indade. It's years now that I've been wanting to do it. And there I was on a roof in Dublin and who should I see coming down the street but my brother and I there with a rifle in my hand. A lovely shot it was, though I say it myself. Picked him off as clean as a bird. Ah! It was a foine moment, that, and I'll never forget it!'"

Boyd Carrington told a story well, with exaggerated dramatic emphasis, and we all laughed and felt easier. When he got up and strolled off saying he must get a bath before dinner, Norton voiced our feeling by saying with enthusiasm:

"What a splendid chap he is!"

I agreed, and Luttrell said: "Yes, yes, a good fellow."

"Always been a success everywhere, so I understand," said Norton. "Everything he's turned his hand to has succeeded. Clear-headed, knows his own mind—essentially a man of action. The true successful man."

Luttrell said slowly:

"Some men are like that. Everything they turn their hand to succeeds. They can't go wrong. Some people—have all the luck."

Norton gave a quick shake of the head.

"No, no, sir. Not luck." He quoted with meaning. "Not in our stars, dear Brutus—but in ourselves."

Luttrell said: "Perhaps you're right."

I said quickly:

"At any rate he's lucky to have inherited Knatton. What a place! But he certainly ought to marry. He'll be lonely there by himself."

Norton laughed. "Marry and settle down? And suppose his wife bullies him—"

It was the purest bad luck. The sort of remark that anyone could make. But it was unfortunate in the circumstances, and Norton realized it just at the moment that the words came out. He tried to catch them back, hesitated, stammered, and stopped awkwardly. It made the whole thing worse.

Both he and I began to speak at once. I made some idiotic remark about the evening light. Norton said something about having some bridge after dinner.

Colonel Luttrell took no notice of either of us. He said in a queer, inexpressive voice:

"No, Boyd Carrington won't get bullied by his wife. He's not the sort of man who *lets* himself get bullied. *He's* all right. He's a *man!*"

It was very awkward. Norton began babbling about bridge again. In the middle of it a large wood pigeon came flapping over our heads and settled on the branch of a tree not far away.

Colonel Luttrell picked up his gun.

"There's one of the blighters," he said.

But before he could take aim the bird had flown off again through the trees where it was impossible to get a shot at it.

At the same moment, however, the Colonel's attention was diverted by a movement on the far slope.

"Damme, there's a rabbit nibbling the bark of those young fruit trees. Thought I'd wired the place."

He raised the rifle and fired, and as I saw—

There came a scream in a woman's voice. It died in a kind of horrible gurgle.

The rifle fell from the Colonel's hand, his body sagged—he caught his lip.

"My God—it's Daisy."

I was already running across the lawn. Norton came behind me. I reached the spot and knelt down. It was Mrs. Luttrell. She had been kneeling, tying a stake against one of the small fruit trees. The grass was long there so that I realized how it was that the Colonel had not seen her clearly and had only distinguished movement in the grass. The light, too, was confusing. She had been shot through the shoulder and the blood was gushing out.

I bent to examine the wound and looked up at Norton. He was leaning against a tree and was looking green and as though he were going to be sick. He said apologetically:

"I can't stand blood."

I said sharply:

"Get hold of Franklin—at once. Or the nurse."

He nodded and ran off.

It was Nurse Craven who appeared first upon the scene. She was there in an incredibly short time and at once set about in a businesslike way to stop the bleeding. Franklin arrived at a run soon afterwards. Between them they got Mrs. Luttrell into the house and to bed. Franklin dressed and bandaged the wound and sent for her own doctor and Nurse Craven stayed with her.

I ran across Franklin just as he left the telephone.

"How is she?"

"Oh! She'll pull through all right. It missed any vital spot luckily. How did it happen?"

I told him. He said:

"I see. Where's the old boy? He'll be feeling knocked out. I shouldn't wonder. Probably needs attention more than she does. I shouldn't say his heart is any too good."

We found Colonel Luttrell in the smoking room. He was a blue colour round the mouth and looked completely dazed. He said brokenly:

"Daisy? Is she—how is she?"

Franklin said quickly:

"She'll be all right, sir. You needn't worry."

"I—thought—rabbit—nibbling the bark—don't know how I came to make such a mistake. Light in my eyes."

"These things happen," said Franklin drily. "I've seen one or two of them in my time. Look here, sir, you'd better let me give you a pick-me-up. You're not feeling too good."

"I'm all right. Can I—can I go to her?"

"Not just now. Nurse Craven is with her. But you don't need to worry. She's all right. Dr. Oliver will be here presently and he'll tell you the same."

I left the two of them together and went out into the evening sunshine. Judith and Allerton were coming along the path towards me. His head was bent to hers and they were both laughing.

Coming on top of the tragedy that had just happened, it made me feel very angry. I called sharply to Judith and she looked up surprised. In a few words I told them what had occurred.

"What an extraordinary thing to happen," was my daughter's comment.

She did not seem nearly as perturbed as she should have done, I thought.

Allerton's manner was outrageous. He seemed to take the whole thing as a good joke.

"Serves the old harridan damn well right," he observed. "Think the old boy did it on purpose."

"Certainly not," I said sharply. "It was an accident."

"Yes, but I know these accidents. Damned convenient sometimes. My word, if the old boy shot her deliberately, I take off my hat to him."

"It was nothing of the kind," I said angrily.

"Don't be too sure. I've known two men who shot their wives. Cleaning his revolver one was. The other fired point-blank at her as a joke, he said. Didn't know the thing was loaded. Got away with it, both of them. Damned good release, I should say myself."

"Colonel Luttrell," I said coldly, "isn't that type of man."

"Well, you couldn't say it wouldn't be a blessed release, could you?" demanded Allerton pertinently. "They hadn't just had a row or anything, had they?"

I turned away angrily, at the same time trying to hide a certain perturbation. Allerton had come a little too near the mark. For the first time a doubt crept into my mind.

It was not bettered by meeting Boyd Carrington. He had been for a stroll down towards the lake, he explained. When I told him the news, he said at once:

"You don't think he meant to shoot her, do you, Hastings?"

"My dear man."

"Sorry, sorry. I shouldn't have said that. It was only, for the moment, one wondered . . . She— she gave him a bit of provocation, you know."

We were both silent for a moment as we re-

membered the scene we had so unwillingly overheard.

I went upstairs feeling unhappy and worried and
rapped on Poirot's door.

He had already heard through Curtiss of what
had occurred, but he was eager for full details.
Since my arrival at Styles I had got into the way
of reporting most of my daily encounters and conversations in full detail. In this way I felt that the
dear old fellow felt less cut off. It gave him the
illusion of actually participating in everything that
went on. I have always had a good and accurate
memory and found it a simple matter to repeat
conversations verbatim.

Poirot listened very attentively. I was hoping
that he would be able definitely to pooh-pooh the
dreadful suggestion that had by now taken uneasy
control of my mind, but before he had a chance
of telling me what he thought, there came a light
tap on the door.

It was Nurse Craven. She apologized for disturbing us.

"I'm so sorry, but I thought Doctor was here.
The old lady is conscious now and she's worrying
about her husband. She'd like to see him. Do you
know where he is, Captain Hastings? I don't want
to leave my patient."

I volunteered to go and look for him. Poirot
nodded approval and Nurse Craven thanked me
warmly.

I found Colonel Luttrell in a little morning room

that was seldom used. He was standing by the window looking out.

He turned sharply as I came in. His eyes asked a question. He looked, I thought, afraid.

"Your wife is conscious, Colonel Luttrell, and is asking for you."

"Oh." The colour surged up in his cheeks and I realized then how very white he had been before. He said slowly, fumblingly, like an old, old man:

"She—she—is asking for me? I'll—I'll come—at once."

He was so unsteady as he began shuffling towards the door that I came and helped him. He leaned on me heavily as we went up the stairs. His breathing was coming with difficulty. The shock, as Franklin had prophesied, was severe.

We came to the door of the sickroom. I tapped and Nurse Craven's brisk, efficient voice called "Come in."

Still supporting the old man, I went with him into the room. There was a screen round the bed. We came round the corner of it.

Mrs. Luttrell was looking very ill—white and frail, her eyes closed. She opened them as we came round the corner of the screen.

She said in a small breathless voice:

"George—George—"

"Daisy—my dear . . ."

One of her arms was bandaged and supported. The other, the free one, moved unsteadily towards him. He took a step forward and clasped her frail little hand in his. He said again:

"Daisy . . ." And then, gruffly, "Thank God, you're all right."

And looking up at him, seeing his eyes slightly misty, and the deep love and anxiety in them, I felt bitterly ashamed of all our ghoulish imaginings.

I crept quietly out of the room. Camouflaged accident indeed! There was no disguising that heartfelt note of thankfulness. I felt immeasurably relieved.

The sound of the gong startled me as I went along the passage. I had completely forgotten the passage of time. The accident had upset everything. Only the cook had gone on as usual and produced dinner at the usual time.

Most of us had not changed and Colonel Luttrell did not appear. But Mrs. Franklin, looking quite attractive in a pale pink evening dress, was downstairs for once and seemed in good health and spirits. Franklin, I thought, was moody and absorbed.

After dinner, to my annoyance, Allerton and Judith disappeared into the garden together. I sat around a while, listening to Franklin and Norton discussing tropical diseases. Norton was a sympathetic and interested listener, even if he knew little of the subject under discussion.

Mrs. Franklin and Boyd Carrington were talking

at the other end of the room. He was showing her some patterns of curtains or cretonnes.

Elizabeth Cole had a book and seemed deeply absorbed in it. I fancied that she was slightly embarrassed and ill at ease with me. Perhaps not unnaturally so after her confidences of the afternoon. I was sorry about it, all the same, and hoped she did not regret all she had told me. I should have liked to have made it clear to her that I should respect her confidence and not repeat it. However, she gave me no chance.

After a while I went up to Poirot.

I found Colonel Luttrell sitting in the circle of light thrown by the one small electric lamp that was turned on.

He was talking and Poirot was listening. I think the Colonel was speaking to himself rather than to his listener.

"I remember so well—yes, it was at a hunt ball. She wore white stuff, called tulle, I think it was. Floated all round her. Such a pretty girl—bowled me over then and there. I said to myself, 'That's the girl I'm going to marry.' And by Jove, I brought it off. Awfully pretty way she had with her—saucy, you know, plenty of back chat. Always gave as good as she got, bless her."

He chuckled.

I saw the scene in my mind's eye. I could imagine Daisy Luttrell with a young saucy face and that smart tongue—so charming then, so apt to turn shrewish with the years.

But it was as that young girl, his first real love, that Colonel Luttrell was thinking of her tonight. His Daisy.

And again I felt ashamed of what we had said such a few hours previously.

Of course, when Colonel Luttrell had at last taken himself off to bed, I blurted out the whole thing to Poirot.

He listened very quietly. I could make nothing of the expression on his face.

"So that is what you thought, Hastings—that the shot was fired on purpose?"

"Yes. I feel ashamed now—"

Poirot waved aside my present feelings.

"Did the thought occur to you of your own accord, or did someone else suggest it to you?"

"Allerton said something of the kind," I said resentfully. "He would, of course."

"Anyone else?"

"Boyd Carrington suggested it."

"Ah! Boyd Carrington."

"And after all, he's a man of the world and has experience of these things."

"Oh, quite so, quite so. He did not see the thing happen, though?"

"No, he'd gone for a walk. Bit of exercise before changing for dinner."

"I see."

I said uneasily:

"I don't think I really believed that theory. It was only—"

Poirot interrupted me.

"You need not be so remorseful about your suspicions, Hastings. It was an idea quite likely to occur to anyone given the circumstances. Oh yes, it was all quite natural."

There was something in Poirot's manner I did not quite understand. A reserve. His eyes were watching me with a curious expression.

I said slowly:

"Perhaps. But seeing now how devoted he really is to her—"

Poirot nodded.

"Exactly. That is often the case, remember. Underneath the quarrels, the misunderstandings, the apparent hostility of everyday life, a real and true affection can exist."

I agreed. I remembered the gentle, affectionate look in little Mrs. Luttrell's eyes as she looked up at her husband stooping over her bed. No more vinegar, no impatience, no ill temper.

Married life, I mused, as I went to bed, was a curious thing.

That something in Poirot's manner still worried me. That curious watchful look—as though he were waiting for me to see—what?

I was just getting into bed when it came to me. Hit me bang between the eyes.

If Mrs. Luttrell had been killed, it would have been a case like those other cases. Colonel Luttrell would, apparently, have killed his wife. It would have been accounted an accident, yet at the same time nobody would have been sure that it was an accident, or whether it had been done on purpose. Insufficient evidence to show it as murder, but quite enough evidence for murder to be suspected.

But that meant—that meant—

What did it mean?

It meant—if anything at all was to make sense —that it was *not* Colonel Luttrell who shot Mrs. Luttrell, but X.

And that was clearly impossible. I had seen the whole thing. It was Colonel Luttrell who had fired the shot. No other shot had been fired.

Unless— But surely that would be impossible. No, perhaps not impossible—merely highly improbable. But possible, yes . . . Supposing that someone else had waited his moment and, at the exact instant when Colonel Luttrell had fired (at a rabbit), this other person had fired at Mrs. Luttrell. Then only the one shot would have been heard. Or, even with a slight discrepancy, it would have been put down as an echo. (Now I come to think of it, there had been an echo, surely.)

But no, that was absurd. There were ways of deciding exactly what weapon a bullet had been fired from. The marks on the bullet must agree with the rifling of the barrel.

But that, I remembered, was only when the police were anxious to establish what weapon had fired the shot. There would have been no enquiry in this business. For Colonel Luttrell would have been quite as certain as everyone else that it was he who had fired the fatal shot. That fact would have been admitted, accepted without question, there would have been no question of tests. The only doubt would have been whether the shot was fired accidentally or with criminal intent—a question that could never be resolved.

And therefore the case fell into line exactly with those other cases—with the case of the labourer Riggs, who didn't remember but supposed he must have done it; with Maggie Litchfield, who went out of her mind and gave herself up—for a crime she had not committed.

Yes, this case fell into line with the rest and I knew now the meaning of Poirot's manner. He was waiting for me to appreciate the fact.

TEN

I opened the subject with Poirot the following morning. His face lighted up and he wagged his head appreciatively.

"Excellent, Hastings. I wondered if you would see the similarity. I did not want to prompt you, you understand."

"Then I am right. This is another X case?"

"Undeniably."

"But *why*, Poirot? What is the motive?"

Poirot shook his head.

"Don't you know? Haven't you any idea?"

Poirot said slowly:

"I have an idea, yes."

"You've got the connection between all these different cases?"

"I think so."

"Well, then."

I could hardly restrain my impatience.

"No, Hastings."

"But I've got to know."

"It is much better that you should not."

"Why?"

"You must take it from me that it is so."

"You are incorrigible," I said. "Twisted up with arthritis. Sitting here helpless. And still trying to play a 'lone hand.'"

"Do not figure to yourself that I am playing a lone hand. Not at all. You are, on the contrary, very much in the picture, Hastings. You are my eyes and my ears. I only refuse to give you information that might be dangerous."

"To me?"

"To the murderer."

"You want him," I said slowly, "not to suspect that you are on his track? That is it, I suppose. Or else you think that I cannot take care of myself."

"You should at least know one thing, Hastings. A man who has killed once will kill again—and again and again and again."

"At any rate," I said grimly, "there hasn't been another murder this time. One bullet at least has gone wide."

"Yes, that was very fortunate—very fortunate indeed. As I told you, these things are difficult to foresee."

He sighed. His face took on a worried expression.

I went away quietly, realizing sadly how unfit Poirot was now for any sustained effort. His brain was still keen, but he was a sick and tired man.

Poirot had warned me not to try to penetrate the personality of X. In my own mind I still clung to my belief that I had penetrated that personality. There was only one person at Styles who struck me as definitely evil. By a simple question, however, I could make sure of one thing. The test would be a negative one, but would nevertheless have a certain value.

I tackled Judith after breakfast.

"Where had you been yesterday evening when I met you, you and Major Allerton?"

The trouble is that when you are intent on one aspect of a thing, you tend to ignore all other aspects. I was quite startled when Judith flared out at me.

"Really, Father, I don't see what business it is of yours."

I stared at her, rather taken aback.

"I—I only asked."

"Yes, but *why*? Why do you have to be continually asking questions? What was I doing? Where did I go? Who was I with? It's really intolerable!"

The funny part of it was, of course, that this time I was not really asking at all where Judith was. It was Allerton I was interested in.

I tried to pacify her.

"Really, Judith, I don't see why I can't ask a simple question."

"I don't see why you want to know."

"I don't particularly. I mean, I just wondered why neither of you—er—seemed to know what had happened."

"About the accident, do you mean? I'd been down to the village, if you must know, to get some stamps."

I pounced on the personal pronoun.

"Allerton wasn't with you then?"

Judith gave an exasperated gasp.

"No, he was not," she said in tones of cold fury. "Actually we'd met just near the house and only about two minutes before we met you. I hope you're satisfied now. But I'd just like to say that if I'd spent the whole day walking around with Major Allerton, it's really not your business. I'm twenty-one and earning my own living and how I spend my time is entirely my own business."

"Entirely," I said quickly, trying to stem the tide.

"I'm glad you agree." Judith looked mollified. She gave a rueful half smile. "Oh, dearest, do try and not come the heavy father quite so much. You don't know how maddening it is. If you just wouldn't *fuss* so."

"I won't—I really won't in future," I promised her.

Franklin came striding along at this minute.

"Hullo, Judith. Come along. We're later than usual."

His manner was curt and really hardly polite. In spite of myself I felt annoyed. I knew that Franklin was Judith's employer, that he had a call upon her time and that, since he paid for it, he was entitled to give her orders. Nevertheless I did not see why he could not behave with common courtesy. His manners were not what one would call polished to anyone, but he did at least behave to most people with a certain amount of everyday politeness. But to Judith, especially of late, his manner was always curt and dictatorial in the extreme. He hardly looked at her when he spoke and merely barked out orders. Judith never appeared to resent this, but I did on her behalf. It crossed my mind that it was especially unfortunate since it contrasted in such a very marked way with Allerton's exaggerated attention. No doubt John Franklin was a ten times better man than Allerton, but he compared very badly with him from the point of view of attraction.

I watched Franklin as he strode along the path towards the laboratory, his ungainly walk, his angular build, the jutting bones of his face and head, his red hair and his freckles. An ugly man and an ungainly man. None of the more obvious qualities. A good brain, yes, but women seldom fall for brains alone. I reflected with dismay that Judith, owing to the circumstances of her job, practically never came into contact with other men. She had no opportunity of sizing up various attractive men. Compared with the gruff and unattractive Franklin, Allerton's meretricious charms stood out with all the force of contrast. My poor girl had no chance of appraising him at his true worth.

Supposing that she should come seriously to lose her heart to him? The irritability she had shown just now was a disquieting sign. Allerton, I knew, was a real bad lot. He was possibly something more. If Allerton were X—?

He could be. At the time that the shot was fired, he had not been with Judith.

But what was the motive of all these seemingly purposeless crimes? There was, I felt sure, nothing of the madman about Allerton. He was sane—altogether sane—and utterly unprincipled.

And Judith—my Judith—was seeing altogether too much of him.

II

Up to this time, though I had been faintly worried about my daughter, my preoccupation over X and the possibility of a crime occurring at any moment had successfully driven more personal problems to the back of my mind.

Now that the blow had fallen, that a crime had been attempted and had mercifully failed, I was free to reflect on these things. And the more I did so, the more anxious I became. A chance word spoken one day revealed to me the fact that Allerton was a married man.

Boyd Carrington, who knew all about everyone, enlightened me further. Allerton's wife was a devout Roman Catholic. She had left him a short time after their marriage. Owing to her religion there had never been any question of divorce.

"And if you ask me," said Boyd Carrington frankly, "it suits the blighter down to the ground. His intentions are always dishonourable, and a wife in the background suits the book very well."

Pleasant hearing for a father!

The days after the shooting accident passed uneventfully enough on the surface, but they accompanied a growing undercurrent of unrest on my part.

Colonel Luttrell spent much time in his wife's bedroom. A nurse had arrived to take charge of the patient and Nurse Craven was able to resume her ministrations to Mrs. Franklin.

Without wishing to be ill-natured, I must admit that I had observed signs on Mrs. Franklin's part of irritation at not being the invalid *en chef*. The fuss and attention that centred round Mrs. Luttrell was clearly very displeasing to the little lady who was accustomed to her own health being the main topic of the day.

She lay about in a hammock chair, her hand to her side, complaining of palpitations. No food that was served was suitable for her, and all her exactions were masked by a veneer of patient endurance.

"I do so hate making a fuss," she murmured plaintively to Poirot. "I feel so ashamed of my wretched health. It's so—so *humiliating* always to have to ask people to be doing things for me. I sometimes think ill health is really a crime. If one isn't healthy and insensitive, one isn't fit for this world and one should just be put quietly away."

"Ah no, madame." Poirot, as always, was gallant. "The delicate exotic flower has to have the shelter of the greenhouse—it cannot endure the cold winds. It is the common weed that thrives in the wintry air—but it is not to be prized higher on that account. Consider my case—cramped, twisted, unable to move, but I—I do not think of quitting life. I enjoy still what I can—the food, the drink, the pleasures of the intellect."

Mrs. Franklin sighed and murmured:

"Ah, but it's different for you. You have no one but yourself to consider. In my case, there is my poor John. I feel acutely what a burden I am to him. A sickly useless wife. A millstone hung round his neck."

"He has never said that you are that, I am sure."

"Oh, not *said* so. Of course not. But men are so transparent, poor dears. And John isn't any good at concealing his feelings. He doesn't mean, of course, to be unkind, but he's—well, mercifully for himself he's a very insensitive sort of person.

He's no feelings and so he doesn't expect anyone else to have them. It's so terribly lucky to be born thick-skinned."

"I should not describe Dr. Franklin as thick-skinned."

"Wouldn't you? Oh, but you don't know him as well as I do. Of course I know that if it wasn't for me, he would be much freer. Sometimes, you know, I get so terribly depressed that I think what a relief it would be to end it all."

"Oh, come, madame."

"After all, what use am I to anybody? To go out of it all into the Great Unknown—" She shook her head. "And then John would be free."

"Great fiddlesticks," said Nurse Craven when I repeated this conversation to her. "She won't do anything of the kind. Don't you worry, Captain Hastings. These ones that talk about 'ending it all' in a dying duck voice haven't the faintest intention of doing anything of the kind."

And I must say that once the excitement aroused by Mrs. Luttrell's injury had died down and Nurse Craven was once more in attendance, Mrs. Franklin's spirits improved very much.

On a particularly fine morning Curtiss had taken Poirot down to the corner below the beech trees near the laboratory. This was a favourite spot of his. It was sheltered from any east wind and in fact hardly any breeze could ever be felt there. This suited Poirot, who abhorred draughts and was always suspicious of the fresh air. Actually, I think, he much preferred to be indoors but had grown to tolerate the outer air when muffled in rugs.

I strolled down to join him there, and just as I got there, Mrs. Franklin came out of the laboratory.

She was most becomingly dressed and looked remarkably cheerful. She explained that she was driving over with Boyd Carrington to see the house and to give expert advice on choosing cretonnes.

"I left my handbag in the lab yesterday when I was talking to John," she explained. "Poor John, he and Judith have driven into Tadcaster—they were short of some chemical reagent or other."

She sank down on a seat near Poirot and shook her head with a comical expression. "Poor dears— I'm so glad I haven't got the scientific mind. On a lovely day like this—it—all seems so puerile."

"You must not let scientists hear you say that, madame."

"No, of course not." Her face changed. It grew serious. She said quietly:

"You mustn't think, M. Poirot, that I don't admire my husband. I do. I think the way he just lives for his work is really—tremendous."

There was a little tremor in her voice.

A suspicion crossed my mind that Mrs. Franklin rather liked playing different roles. At this moment she was being the loyal and hero-worshipping wife.

She leaned forward, placing an earnest hand on Poirot's knee.

"John," she said, "is really a—a kind of *saint*. It makes me quite frightened sometimes."

To call Franklin a saint was somewhat overstating the case, I thought, but Barbara Franklin went on, her eyes shining:

"He'll do anything—take any risk—just to advance the sum of human knowledge. That is pretty fine, don't you think?"

"Assuredly, assuredly," said Poirot quickly.

"But sometimes, you know," went on Mrs. Franklin, "I'm really nervous about him. The lengths to which he'll go, I mean. This horrid bean thing he's experimenting with now. I'm so afraid that he'll start experimenting on himself."

"He'd take every precaution, surely," I said.

She shook her head with a slight, rueful smile.

"You don't know John. Did you ever hear about what he did with that new gas?"

I shook my head.

"It was some new gas they wanted to find out about. John volunteered to test it. He was shut up in a tank for something like thirty-six hours—taking his pulse and temperature and respiration—to see what the aftereffects were and if they were the same for men as for animals. It was a frightful risk, so one of the professors told me afterwards. He might easily have passed out altogether. But that's the sort of person John is—absolutely oblivious of his own safety. I think it's rather wonderful, don't you, to be like that? *I* should never be brave enough."

"It needs, indeed, high courage," said Poirot, "to do these things in cold blood."

Barbara Franklin said:

"Yes, it does. I'm awfully proud of him, you know, but at the same time it makes me rather nervous, too. Because, you see, guinea pigs and frogs are no good after a certain point. You want the human reaction. That's why I feel so terrified that John will go and dose himself with this nasty ordeal bean and that something awful might happen." She sighed and shook her head. "But he only laughs at my fears. He really *is* a sort of saint, you know."

At this moment Boyd Carrington came towards us.

"Hullo, Babs, ready?"

"Yes, Bill, waiting for you."

"I do hope it won't tire you too much."

"Of course it won't. I feel better today than I have for ages."

She got up, smiled prettily at us both, and walked up the lawn with her tall escort.

"Dr. Franklin—the modern saint—h'm," said Poirot.

"Rather a change of attitude," I said. "But I think the lady is like that."

"Like what?"

"Given to dramatizing herself in various roles. One day the misunderstood neglected wife, then the self-sacrificing suffering woman who hates to be a burden on the man she loves. Today it's the hero-worshipping helpmate. The trouble is that all the roles are slightly overdone."

Poirot said thoughtfully:

"You think Mrs. Franklin, do you not, rather a fool?"

"Well, I wouldn't say that—yes, perhaps not a very brilliant intellect."

"Ah, she is not your type."

"Who is my type?" I snapped.

Poirot replied unexpectedly:

"Open your mouth and shut your eyes and see what the fairies will send you—"

I was prevented from replying because Nurse Craven came tripping hastily across the grass. She gave us a smile with a brilliant flash of teeth, unlocked the door of the lab, passed inside and reappeared with a pair of gloves.

"First a hanky and now gloves, always something left behind," she observed as she sped back with them to where Barbara Franklin and Boyd Carrington were waiting.

Mrs. Franklin, I reflected, was that rather feckless type of woman who always did leave things behind, shedding her possessions and expecting everybody to retrieve them as a matter of course, and even, I fancied, was rather proud of herself for so doing. I had heard her more than once murmur complacently:

"Of course I've got a head like a *sieve*."

I sat looking after Nurse Craven as she ran across the lawn and out of sight. She ran well, her body was vigorous and well balanced. I said impulsively:

"I should think a girl must get fed up with that sort of life. I mean when there isn't much nursing to be done—when it's just fetch and carry. I don't suppose Mrs. Franklin is particularly considerate or kindly."

Poirot's response was distinctly annoying. For no reason whatever, he closed his eyes and murmured:

"Auburn hair."

Undoubtedly Nurse Craven had auburn hair—but I did not see why Poirot should choose just this minute to comment upon it.

I made no reply.

ELEVEN

It was, I think, on the following morning before lunch that a conversation took place which left me vaguely disquieted.

There were four of us—Judith, myself, Boyd Carrington and Norton.

Exactly how the subject started, I am not sure, but we were talking of euthanasia—the case for and against it.

Boyd Carrington, as was natural, did most of the talking, Norton putting in a word or two here and there, and Judith sitting silent but closely attentive.

I myself had confessed that though there seemed, on the face of it, every reason to support the practice, yet in actuality I felt a sentimental shrinking from it. Besides, I said, I thought it would put too much power in the hands of relatives.

Norton agreed with me. He added that he thought it should only be done by the wish and consent of the patient himself where death after prolonged suffering was certain.

Boyd Carrington said:

"Ah, but that's the curious thing. Does the person most concerned ever wish to 'put himself out of his misery,' as we say?"

He then told a story, which he said was authentic, of a man in terrible pain from inoperable cancer. This man had begged the doctor in attendance to "give him something that would finish it all." The doctor had replied: "I can't do that, old man." Later, on leaving, he had placed by the patient some morphia tablets, telling him carefully how many he could safely take and what dose would be dangerous. Although these were left in the patient's charge and he could easily have taken a fatal quantity, he did not do so, "thus proving," said Boyd Carrington, "that, in spite of his words, the man preferred his suffering to a swift and merciful release."

It was then that Judith spoke for the first time, spoke with vigour and abruptly:

"Of course he would," she said. "It shouldn't have been left to him to decide."

Boyd Carrington asked what she meant.

"I mean that anyone who's weak—in pain and ill—hasn't got the strength to make a decision.

They can't. It must be done for them. It's the duty of someone who loves them to make the decision."

"Duty?" I queried dubiously.

Judith turned on me.

"Yes, *duty*. Someone whose mind is clear and who will take the responsibility."

Boyd Carrington shook his head.

"And end up on the dock charged with murder?"

"Not necessarily. Anyway, if you love someone, you would take the risk."

"But look here, Judith," said Norton. "What you're suggesting is simply a terrific responsibility to take."

"I don't think it is. People are too afraid of responsibility. They'll take responsibility where a dog is concerned—why not with a human being?"

"Well—it's rather different, isn't it?"

Judith said:

"Yes, it's more important."

Norton murmured:

"You take my breath away."

Boyd Carrington asked curiously:

"So *you'd* take the risk, would you?"

"I think so," said Judith. "I'm not afraid of taking risks."

Boyd Carrington shook his head.

"It wouldn't do, you know. You can't have people here, there, and everywhere taking the law into their own hands. Deciding matters of life and death."

Norton said:

"Actually, you know, Boyd Carrington, most people wouldn't have the nerve to take the responsibility."

He smiled faintly as he looked at Judith.

"Don't believe you would if it came to the point."

Judith said composedly:

"One can't be sure, of course. I think I should."

Norton said with a slight twinkle:

"Not unless you had an axe of your own to grind."

Judith flushed hotly. She said sharply:

"That just shows you don't understand at all. If I had a—a personal motive, I couldn't do anything. Don't you see?" she appealed to us all. "It's got to be absolutely impersonal. You could only take the responsibility of—of ending a life if you were quite sure of your motive. It must be absolutely selfless."

"All the same," said Norton, "you wouldn't do it."

Judith insisted:

"I would. To begin with I don't hold life as sacred as all you people do. Unfit lives, useless lives—they should be got out of the way. There's so much *mess* about. Only people who can make a decent contribution to the community ought to be allowed to live. The others ought to be put painlessly away."

She appealed suddenly to Boyd Carrington.

"You agree with me, don't you?"

He said slowly:

"In principle, yes. Only the worthwhile should survive."

"Wouldn't you take the law into your own hands if it was necessary?"

Boyd Carrington said slowly:

"Perhaps. I don't know ..."

Norton said quietly:

"A lot of people would agree with you in theory. But practice is a different matter."

"That's not logical."

Norton said impatiently:

"Of course it's not. It's really a question of *courage*. One just hasn't got the *guts*—to put it vulgarly."

Judith was silent. Norton went on:

"Frankly, you know, Judith, you'd be just the same yourself. You wouldn't have the courage when it came to it."

"Don't you think so?"

"I'm sure of it."

"I think you're wrong, Norton," said Boyd Carrington. "I think Judith has any amount of courage. Fortunately the issue doesn't often present itself."

The gong sounded from the house.

Judith got up.

She said very distinctly to Norton:

"You're wrong, you know. I've got more—more guts than you think."

She went swiftly towards the house. Boyd Carrington followed her, saying:

"Hey, wait for me, Judith."

I followed, feeling for some reason rather dismayed. Norton, who was always quick to sense a mood, endeavoured to console me.

"She doesn't mean it, you know," he said. "It's the sort of half-baked idea one has when one is young—but fortunately one doesn't carry it out. It remains just talk."

I think Judith overheard, for she cast a furious glance over her shoulder.

Norton dropped his voice.

"Theories needn't worry anybody," he said. "But look here, Hastings—"

"Yes?"

Norton seemed rather embarrassed. He said:

"I don't want to butt in, but what do you know of Allerton?"

"Of Allerton?"

"Yes, sorry if I'm being a Nosy Parker, but frankly—if I were you, I shouldn't let that girl of yours see too much of him. He's—well, his reputation isn't very good."

"I can see for myself the sort of rotter he is," I said bitterly. "But it's not so easy in these days."

"Oh, I know. Girls can look after themselves, as the saying goes. Most of them can, too. But—well —Allerton has rather a special technique in that line."

He hesitated, then said:

"Look here, I feel I ought to tell you. Don't let it go further, of course—but I do happen to know something pretty foul about him."

He told it me then and there—and I was able to verify it in every detail later. It was a revolting tale. The story of a girl, sure of herself, modern, independent. Allerton had brought all his "technique" to bear upon her. Later had come the other side of the picture—the story ended with a desperate girl taking her own life with an overdose of Veronal.

And the horrible part was that the girl in question had been of much the same type as Judith— the independent highbrow kind. The kind of girl who when she does lose her heart, loses it with a desperation and an abandonment that the silly little fluffy type can never know.

I went in to lunch with a horrible sense of foreboding.

TWELVE

"Is anything worrying you, *mon ami?*" asked Poirot that afternoon.

I did not answer, merely shook my head. I felt that I had no right to burden Poirot with this, my purely personal problem. It was not as though he could help in any way.

Judith would have treated any remonstrances on his part with the smiling detachment of the young towards the boring counsels of the old.

Judith, my Judith . . .

It is hard now to describe just what I went through that day. Afterwards, thinking it over, I am inclined to put something down to the atmosphere of Styles itself. Evil imaginings came easily to the mind there. There was, too, not only the past, but a sinister present. The shadow of murder and a murderer haunted the house.

And to the best of my belief the murderer was Allerton, and Judith was losing her heart to him! It was all unbelievable—monstrous—and I didn't know what to do.

It was after lunch that Boyd Carrington drew me aside. He hemmed and hawed a bit before coming to the point. At last he said rather jerkily:

"Don't think I'm interfering, but I think you ought to speak to that girl of yours. Give her a word of warning—eh? You know this fellow Allerton—reputation's pretty bad, and she—well, it looks rather like a case."

So easy for these men without children to speak like that! Give her a word of warning?

Would it be any use? Would it make things worse?

If only Cinders were here. She would know what to do—what to say.

I was tempted, I admit, to hold my peace and say nothing. But I reflected after a while that this was really only cowardice. I shrank from the unpleasantness of having things out with Judith. I was, you see, afraid of my tall, beautiful daughter.

I paced up and down the gardens in increasing agitation of mind. My footsteps led me at last to the rose garden, and there, as it were, the decision was taken out of my hands, for Judith was sitting on a seat alone, and in all my life I have never seen an expression of greater unhappiness on any woman's face.

The mask was off. Indecision and deep unhappiness showed only too plainly.

I took my courage in my hands. I went to her. She did not hear me until I was beside her.

"Judith," I said. "For God's sake, Judith, don't mind so much."

She turned on me, startled.

"Father? I didn't hear you."

I went on, knowing that it would be fatal if she managed to turn me back to normal everyday conversation.

"Oh, my dearest child, don't think I don't know, that I can't see. He isn't worth it—oh, do believe me, he isn't worth it."

Her face, troubled, alarmed, was turned towards me. She said quietly:

"Do you think you really know what you are talking about?"

"I do know. You care about this man. But, my dear, it's no good."

She smiled sombrely. A heartbreaking smile.

"Perhaps I know that as well as you do."

"You don't. You can't. Oh, Judith, what can come of it all? He's a married man. There can be no future there for you—only sorrow and shame—and all ending in bitter self-loathing."

Her smile grew wider—even more sorrowful.

"How fluently you talk, don't you?"

"Give it up, Judith—give it all up."

"No!"

"He's not worth it, my dear."

She said very quietly and slowly:

"He's worth everything in the world to me."

"No, no. Judith, I beg of you—"

The smile vanished. She turned on me like an avenging fury.

"How dare you? How dare you interfere? I won't stand it. You are never to speak to me of this again. I hate you—I hate you. It's no business of yours. It's *my* life—my own secret inside life!"

She got up. With one firm hand she pushed me aside and went past me. Like an avenging fury. I stared after her—dismayed.

II

I was still there, dazed and helpless, unable to think out my next course of action, some quarter of an hour later.

I was there when Elizabeth Cole and Norton found me.

They were, I realized later, very kind to me. They saw, they must have seen, that I was in a state of great mental perturbation. But tactfully enough they made no slightest allusion to my state of mind. Instead they took me with them on a rambling walk. They were both nature lovers. Elizabeth Cole pointed out wild flowers to me, Norton showed me birds through his field glasses.

Their talk was gentle, soothing, concerned only with feathered beings and with woodland flora. Little by little I came back to normal although underneath I was still in a state of the utmost perturbation.

Moreover I was, as people are, convinced that any happening that occurred was connected with my own particular perplexity.

So, therefore, when Norton, his glasses to his eyes, exclaimed: "Hullo, if that isn't a speckled woodpecker. I never—" and then broke off suddenly, I immediately leapt to suspicion. I held out my hand for the glasses.

"Let me see."

My voice was peremptory.

Norton fumbled with the glasses. He said in a curious hesitating voice:

"I—I—made a mistake—it's flown away—at least, as a matter of fact, it was quite a common bird."

His face was white and troubled. He avoided looking at us. He seemed both bewildered and distressed.

Even now I cannot think I was altogether unreasonable in jumping to the conclusion that he had seen through those glasses of his something that he was determined to prevent my seeing.

Whatever it was that he had seen, he was so thoroughly taken aback by it that it was noticeable to both of us.

His glasses had been trained on a distant belt of woodland. What had he seen there?

I said peremptorily:

"Let me look."

I snatched at the glasses. I remember he tried to defend them from me, but he did it clumsily. I seized them roughly.

Norton said weakly:

"It wasn't really— I mean, the bird's gone . . . I wish—"

My hands shaking a little, I adjusted the glasses to my eyes. They were powerful glasses. I trained them as nearly as I could on the spot where I thought Norton had been looking.

But I saw nothing—nothing but a gleam of white (a girl's white dress?) disappearing into the trees.

I lowered the glasses. Without a word I handed them back to Norton. He did not meet my eyes. He was looking worried and perplexed.

We walked back to the house in silence and I remember that Norton was very silent all the way.

III

Mrs. Franklin and Boyd Carrington came in shortly after we got back to the house. He had taken her in his car to Tadminster because she wanted to do some shopping.

She had done it, I gather, pretty thoroughly. Lots

of parcels came out of the car and she was looking quite animated, talking and laughing and with quite a colour in her cheeks.

She sent Boyd Carrington up with a particularly fragile purchase and I gallantly received a further consignment.

Her talk was quicker and more nervous than usual.

"Frightfully hot, isn't it? I think there's going to be a storm. This weather must break soon. They say, you know, there's quite a water shortage. The worst drought there's been for years."

She went on, turning to Elizabeth Cole:

"What have you all been doing with yourselves? Where's John? He said he'd got a headache and was going to walk it off. Very unlike him to have a headache. I think, you know, he's worried about his experiments. They aren't going right or something. I wish he'd talk more about things."

She paused and then addressed Norton:

"You're very silent, Mr. Norton. Is anything the matter? You look—you look scared. You haven't seen the ghost of old Mrs. Whoever-it-was?"

Norton started.

"No, no. I haven't seen any ghosts. I—I was just thinking of something."

It was at that moment that Curtiss came through the doorway wheeling Poirot in his invalid chair.

He stopped with it in the hall, preparatory to taking his master out and carrying him up the stairs.

153

Poirot, his eyes suddenly alert, looked from one to the other of us.

He said sharply:

"What is it? Is anything the matter?"

None of us answered for a minute, then Barbara Franklin said with a little artificial laugh:

"No, of course not. What should be the matter? It's just—perhaps thunder coming? I—oh, dear— I'm terribly tired. Bring those things up, will you, Captain Hastings. Thank you so much."

I followed her up the stairs and along the east wing. Her room was the end one on that side.

Mrs. Franklin opened the door. I was behind her, my arms full of parcels.

She stopped abruptly in the doorway. By the window Boyd Carrington was having his palm examined by Nurse Craven.

He looked up and laughed a little sheepishly.

"Hullo, I'm having my fortune told. Nurse is no end of a hand reader."

"Really? I had no idea of that." Barbara Franklin's voice was sharp. I had an idea that she was annoyed with Nurse Craven. "Please take these things, Nurse, will you? And you might mix me an egg flip. I feel very tired. A hot water bottle, too, please. I'll get to bed as soon as possible."

"Certainly, Mrs. Franklin."

Nurse Craven moved forward. She showed no signs of anything but professional concern.

Mrs. Franklin said:

"Please go, Bill, I'm terribly tired."

Boyd Carrington looked very concerned.

"Oh, I say, Babs, has it been too much for you? I *am* sorry. What a thoughtless fool I am. I shouldn't have let you overtire yourself."

Mrs. Franklin gave him her angelic martyr's smile.

"I didn't want to say anything. I do hate being *tiresome*."

We two men went out of the room somewhat abashed and left the two women together.

Boyd Carrington said contritely:

"What a damned fool I am. Barbara seemed so bright and gay I forgot all about tiring her. Hope she's not knocked herself out."

I said mechanically:

"Oh, I expect she'll be all right after a night's rest."

He went down the stairs. I hesitated and then went along the other wing towards my own room, and Poirot's. The little man would be expecting me. For the first time I was reluctant to go to him. I had so much to occupy my thoughts, and I still had that dull sick feeling at the pit of my stomach.

I went slowly along the corridor.

From inside Allerton's room I heard voices. I don't think I meant consciously to listen, though I stopped for a minute automatically outside his door. Then, suddenly, the door opened and my daughter Judith came out.

She stopped dead when she saw me. I caught her

by the arm and hustled her along into my room.
I was suddenly intensely angry.

"What do you mean by going to that fellow's
room?"

She looked at me steadily. She showed no anger
now, only complete coldness. For some few sec-
onds she did not reply.

I shook her by the arm.

"I won't have it, I tell you. You don't know what
you are doing."

She said then in a low, biting voice:

"I think you have a perfectly filthy mind."

I said:

"I daresay I have. It's a reproach your generation is fond of levelling at mine. We have, at least,
certain standards. Understand this, Judith, I forbid you absolutely to have anything more to do
with that man."

She looked at me steadily. Then she said quietly:

"I see. So that's it."

"Do you deny that you're in love with him?"

"No."

"But you don't know what he is. You can't
know."

Deliberately, without mincing my language, I
repeated to her the story I had heard about Allerton.

"You see," I said when I had finished. "That's
the kind of foul brute he is."

She seemed quite unmoved. Her lip curled upwards scornfully.

"I never thought he was a saint, I can assure you."

"Doesn't this make any difference to you? Judith, you can't be utterly depraved."

"Call it that if you like."

"Judith, you haven't—you aren't—"

I could not put my meaning into words. She shook her arm free from my detaining hand.

"Now, listen, Father. I do what I choose. You can't bully me. And it's no good ranting. I shall do exactly as I please with my life, and you can't stop me."

In another instant she was out of the room.

I found my knees trembling.

I sank down onto a chair. It was worse—much worse than I thought. The child was utterly infatuated. There was no one to whom I could appeal. Her mother, the only person she might have listened to, was dead. It all depended on me.

I do not think that either before or since, I have ever suffered as I suffered then . . .

IV

Presently I roused myself. I washed and shaved and changed. I went down to dinner. I behaved, I fancy, in quite a normal manner. Nobody seemed to notice anything amiss.

Once or twice I saw Judith flash a curious glance at me. She must have been puzzled, I think, by the way I was able to appear quite like my usual self.

And all the time, underneath, I was growing more and more determined.

All that I needed was courage—courage and brains.

After dinner we went outside, looked up at the sky, commented on the closeness of the atmosphere, prophesied rain—thunder—a storm.

Out of the tail of my eye I saw Judith disappear round the corner of the house. Presently Allerton strolled in the same direction.

I finished what I was saying to Boyd Carrington and wandered that way myself.

Norton, I think, tried to stop me. He took my arm. He tried, I think, to suggest walking up to the rose garden. I took no notice.

He was still with me as I turned the corner of the house.

They were there. I saw Judith's upturned face, saw Allerton's bent down over it—saw how he took her in his arms and the kiss that followed.

Then they broke away quickly. I took a step forward. Almost by main force, Norton hauled me back and round the corner. He said:

"Look here, you can't—"

I interrupted him. I said forcefully:

"I can. And I will."

"It's no *good*, my dear fellow. It's all very distressing, but all it comes to is that there's nothing you *can* do."

I was silent. He might think that that was so, but I knew better.

Norton went on:

"I know how ineffectual and maddened one feels, but the only thing to do is to admit defeat. *Accept* it, man!"

I didn't contradict him. I waited, allowing him to talk. Then I went firmly round the corner of the house again.

The two of them had disappeared now, but I had a shrewd idea of where they might be. There was a summerhouse concealed in a grove of lilac trees not far away.

I went towards it. I think Norton was still with me, but I'm not sure.

As I got nearer, I heard voices and stopped. It was Allerton's voice I heard.

"Well, then, my dear girl, that's settled. Don't make any more objections. You go up to town to-morrow. I'll say I'm running over to Ipswich to stay with a pal for a night or two. You wire from London that you can't get back. And who's to know of that charming little dinner at my flat? You won't regret it, I can promise you."

I felt Norton tugging at me, and suddenly, meekly, I turned. I almost laughed at the sight of his worried, anxious face. I let him drag me back to the house. I pretended to give in because I knew, at that moment, exactly what I was going to do . . .

I said to him clearly and distinctly:

"Don't worry, old chap. It's all no good—I see that now. You can't control your children's lives. I'm through."

He was ridiculously relieved.

Shortly afterwards, I told him I was going to bed early. I'd got a bit of a headache, I said.

He had no suspicions at all of what I was going to do.

V

I paused for a moment in the corridor. It was quite quiet. There was no one about. The beds had been all turned down ready for the night. Norton, who had a room on this side, I had left downstairs. Elizabeth Cole was playing bridge. Curtiss, I knew, would be downstairs having his supper. I had the place to myself.

I flatter myself that I have not worked with Poirot for so many years in vain. I knew just what precautions to take.

Allerton was *not* going to meet Judith in London tomorrow.

Allerton was not going anywhere tomorrow . . .

The whole thing was really so ridiculously simple.

I went to my own room and picked up my bottle of aspirins. Then I went into Allerton's room and into the bathroom. The tablets of Slumberyl were in the cupboard. Eight, I considered, ought to do the trick. One or two was the stated dose. Eight, therefore, ought to be ample. Allerton himself had said the toxic dose was not high. I read the label: "It is dangerous to exceed the prescribed dose."

I smiled to myself.

I wrapped a silk handkerchief round my hand and unscrewed the bottle carefully. There must be no fingerprints on it.

I emptied out the tablets. Yes, they were almost exactly the same size as the aspirins. I put eight aspirins in the bottle, then filled up with the Slumberyls, leaving out eight of them. The bottle now looked exactly as it had before. Allerton would notice no difference.

I went back to my room. I had a bottle of whisky there—most of us had at Styles. I got out two glasses and a siphon. I'd never known Allerton refuse a drink yet. When he came up, I'd ask him in for a nightcap.

I tried the tablets in a little of the spirit. They dissolved easily enough. I tasted the mixture gingerly. A shade bitter perhaps, but hardly noticeable. I had my plan. I should be just pouring myself out a drink when Allerton came up. I would hand that to him and pour myself out another. All quite easy and natural.

He could have no idea of my feelings—unless of course Judith had told him. I considered this for a moment, but decided that I was quite safe here. Judith never told anyone anything.

He would probably believe me to be quite unsuspicious of their plans.

I had nothing to do but to wait. It would be a long time, probably an hour or two before Allerton came up to bed. He was always a late bird.

I sat there quietly waiting.

A sudden knock on the door made me start. It was only Curtiss, however. Poirot was asking for me.

I came to myself with a shock. Poirot! I had never once thought of him all evening. He must have wondered what had become of me. It worried me a little. First of all because I was ashamed of never having been near him, and secondly I did not want him to suspect that anything out of the way had happened.

I followed Curtiss across the passage.

"*Eh bien,*" exclaimed Poirot. "So you desert me, *hein?*"

I forced a yawn and an apologetic smile.

"Awfully sorry, old boy," I said. "But to tell the truth, I've got such a blinding headache I can hardly see out of my eyes. It's the thunder in the air, I suppose. I really have been feeling quite muzzy with it—in fact so much so, I entirely forgot I hadn't been in to say good night to you."

As I had hoped, Poirot was immediately solicitous. He offered remedies. He fussed. He accused me of having sat about in the open air in a draught. (On the hottest day of the summer!) I refused aspirin on the grounds that I had already taken some, but I was not able to avoid being given a cup of sweet and wholly disgusting chocolate!

"It nourishes the nerves, you comprehend," Poirot explained.

I drank it to avoid argument and then, with Poirot's anxious and affectionate exclamations still ringing in my ears, I bade him good night.

I returned to my own room and shut the door ostentatiously. Later, I opened it a crack with the utmost caution. I could not fail now to hear Allerton when he came. But it would be some time yet.

I sat there waiting. I thought of my dead wife. Once, under my breath, I murmured:

"You understand, darling, I'm going to save her."

She had left Judith in my care. I was not going to fail her.

In the quiet and the stillness I suddenly felt that Cinders was very near to me.

I felt almost as though she were in the room.

And still I sat on, grimly waiting.

THIRTEEN

There is something about writing down an anti-climax in cold blood that is somewhat shattering to one's self-esteem.

For the truth of the matter is, you see, that I sat there waiting for Allerton and that I fell asleep!

Not so surprising, really, I suppose. I had slept very badly the night before. I had been out in the air the whole day. I was worn out with worry and the strain of nerving myself for doing what I had decided to do. On top of all that was the heavy thundery weather. Possibly even the fierce effort of concentration I was making helped.

Anyway, it happened. I fell asleep there in my chair, and when I woke, birds were twittering outside, the sun was up and there was I cramped and uncomfortable, slipped down in my chair in my evening dress, with a foul taste in the mouth and a splitting head.

I was bewildered, incredulous, disgusted, and finally immeasurably and overwhelmingly relieved.

Who was it who wrote: "The darkest day (Live till tomorrow) will have pass'd away"? And how true it is. I saw now, clearly and sanely, how overwrought and wrong-headed I had been. Melodramatic, lost to all sense of proportion. I had actually made up my mind to kill another human being.

At this moment my eyes fell on the glass of whisky in front of me. With a shudder I got up, drew the curtains and poured it out of the window. I must have been mad last night!

I shaved, had a bath and dressed. Then, feeling very much better, I went across to Poirot. He always woke very early, I knew. I sat down and made a clean breast of the whole thing to him.

I may say it was a great relief.

He shook his head gently at me.

"Ah, but what follies it is you contemplate. I am glad you came to confess your sins to me. But why, my dear friend, did you not come to me last night and tell me what was in your mind?"

I said shamefacedly:

"I was afraid, I suppose, that you would have tried to stop me."

"Assuredly I would have stopped you. Ah, that, certainly. Do you think I want to see you hanged by the neck, all on account of a very unpleasant scoundrel called Major Allerton?"

"I shouldn't have been caught," I said. "I'd taken every precaution."

"That is what all murderers think. You had the true mentality! But let me tell you, *mon ami*, you were not as clever as you thought yourself."

"I took every precaution. I wiped my finger-prints off the bottle."

"Exactly. You also wiped Allerton's fingerprints off. And when he is found dead—what happens? They perform the autopsy and it is established that he died of an overdose of Slumberyl. Did he take it by accident or intention? *Tiens*, his finger-prints are not on the bottle. But why not? Whether accident or suicide, he would have no reason to wipe them off. And then they analyze the remaining tablets and find nearly half of them have been replaced by aspirin."

"Well, practically everyone has aspirin tablets," I murmured weakly.

"Yes, but it is not everyone who has a daughter whom Allerton is pursuing with dishonourable intentions—to use an old-fashioned melodramatic phrase. And you have had a quarrel with your daughter on the subject the day before. Two people, Boyd Carrington and Norton, can swear to your violent feeling against the man. No, Hastings, it would not have looked too good. Attention would immediately have been focussed upon you, and by that time you would probably have been in such a state of fear—or even remorse, that some good solid inspector of police would have made up his mind quite definitely that you were the guilty party. It is quite possible, even, that someone may have seen you tampering with the tablets."

"They couldn't. There was no one about."

"There is a balcony outside the window. Somebody might have been there, peeping in. Or, who knows, someone might have been looking through the keyhole."

"You've got keyholes on the brain, Poirot. People don't really spend their time looking through keyholes as much as you seem to think."

Poirot half closed his eyes and remarked that I had always had too trusting a nature.

"And let me tell you, very funny things happen with keys in this house. Me, I like to feel that my door is locked on the inside, even if the good Curtiss is in the adjoining room. Soon after I am here, my key disappears—but entirely! I have to have another one made."

"Well, anyway," I said with a deep breath of relief, my mind still laden up with my own troubles, "it didn't come off. It's awful to think one can get worked up like that." I lowered my voice. "Poirot, you don't think that because—because of that murder long ago there's a sort of infection in the air?"

"A virus of murder, you mean? Well, it is an interesting suggestion."

CURTAIN

"Houses do have an atmosphere," I said thoughtfully. "This house has a bad history."

Poirot nodded.

"Yes. There have been people here—several of
them—who desired deeply that someone else
should die. That is true enough."

"I believe it gets hold of one in some way. But
now, Poirot, tell me, what am I to do about all this
—Judith and Allerton, I mean? It's got to be
stopped somehow. What do you think I'd better
do?"

"Do nothing," said Poirot with emphasis.

"Oh, but—"

"Believe me, you will do least harm by not interfering."

"If I were to tackle Allerton—"

"What can you say or do? Judith is twenty-one
and her own mistress."

"But I feel I ought to be able—"

Poirot interrupted me.

"No, Hastings. Do not imagine that you are
clever enough, forceful enough, or even cunning
enough to impose your personality on either of
those two people. Allerton is accustomed to dealing
with angry and impotent fathers, and probably
enjoys it as a good joke. Judith is not the sort of
creature who can be browbeaten. I would advise
you—if I advised you at all—to do something very
different. I would trust her, if I were you."

I stared at him.

"Judith," said Hercule Poirot, "is made of very fine stuff. I admire her very much."

I said, my voice unsteady:

"I admire her, too. But I'm afraid for her."

Poirot nodded his head with sudden energy.

"I, too, am afraid for her," he said. "But not in the way you are. I am terribly afraid. And I am powerless—or nearly so. And the days go by. There is danger, Hastings, and it is very close."

II

I knew as well as Poirot that the danger was very close. I had more reason to know it than he had, because of what I had actually overheard the previous night.

Nevertheless I pondered on that phrase of Poirot's as I went down to breakfast. "I would trust her if I were you."

It had come unexpectedly—but it had given me an odd sense of comfort. And almost immediately, the truth of it was justified. For Judith had obviously changed her mind about going up to London that day.

Instead she went off with Franklin to the lab as usual directly after breakfast, and it was clear that they were to have an arduous and busy day there.

A feeling of intense thanksgiving rushed over me. How mad, how despairing I had been last night. I had assumed—assumed quite certainly that Judith had yielded to Allerton's specious proposals. But it was true, I reflected now, that I had never heard her actually assent. No, she was too fine, too essentially good and true, to give in. She had refused the rendezvous.

Allerton had breakfast early, I found, and gone off to Ipswich. He, then, had kept to the plan and must assume that Judith was going up to London as arranged.

Well, I thought grimly, he would get a disappointment.

Boyd Carrington came along and remarked rather grumpily that I looked very cheerful this morning.

"Yes," I said. "I've had some good news."

He said that it was more than he had. He'd had a tiresome telephone call from the architect, some building difficulty—a local surveyor cutting up rough. Also worrying letters. And he was afraid he'd let Mrs. Franklin overdo herself the day before.

Mrs. Franklin was certainly making up for her recent bout of good health and spirits. She was, so I gathered from Nurse Craven, making herself quite impossible.

Nurse Craven had had to give up her day off which had been promised her to go and meet some friends, and she was decidedly sour about it. Since early morning Mrs. Franklin had been calling for sal volatile, hot water bottles, various patent foods and drinks, and was unwilling to let Nurse leave the room. She had neuralgia, a pain round the heart, cramps in her feet and legs, cold shivers and I don't know what else.

I may say here and now that neither I nor anyone else was inclined to be really alarmed. We all put it down as part of Mrs. Franklin's hypochondriacal tendencies.

This was true of Nurse Craven and Dr. Franklin as well.

The latter was fetched from the laboratory, he listened to his wife's complaints, asked her if she would like the local doctor called in (violently negatived by Mrs. Franklin), he then mixed her a sedative, soothed her as best he could and went off back to work again.

Nurse Craven said to me:

"He knows, of course, she's just playing up."

"You don't really think there's anything much the matter?"

"Her temperature is normal, and her pulse is perfectly good. Just fuss, if you ask me."

She was annoyed and spoke out more imprudently than usual.

"She likes to interfere with anyone else enjoying themselves. She'd like her husband all worked up, and me running round after her, and even Sir William has got to be made to feel a brute because he 'overtired her yesterday.' She's one of that kind."

Nurse Craven was clearly finding her patient almost impossible today. I gathered that Mrs. Franklin had been really extremely rude to her.

She was the kind of woman whom nurses and servants instinctively disliked—not only because of the trouble she gave, but because of her manner of doing so.

So, as I say, none of us took her indisposition seriously.

The only exception was Boyd Carrington, who wandered round looking rather pathetically like a small boy who has been scolded.

How many times since then have I gone over and over the events of that day, trying to remember something so far unheeded—some tiny forgotten incident, striving to remember exactly the manner of everybody. How far they were normal, or showed excitement.

Let me, once more, put down exactly what I remember of everybody.

Boyd Carrington, as I have said, looked uncomfortable and rather guilty. He seemed to think that he had been rather overexuberant the day before and had been selfish in not thinking more of the frail health of his companion. He had been up once or twice to inquire about Barbara Franklin, and Nurse Craven, herself not in the best of tempers, had been tart and snappish with him. He had even been to the village and purchased a box of chocolates. This had been sent down. "Mrs. Franklin couldn't bear chocolates."

Rather disconsolately, he opened the box in the smoking room and Norton and I and he all solemnly helped ourselves.

Norton, I now think, had definitely something on his mind that morning. He was abstracted; once or twice his brows drew together as though he were puzzling over something.

He was fond of chocolates, and ate a good many in an abstracted fashion.

Outside the weather had broken. Since ten o'clock the rain had been pouring down.

It had not the melancholy that sometimes accompanies a wet day. Actually it was a relief to us all.

Poirot had been brought down by Curtiss about midday and ensconced in the drawing room. Here Elizabeth Cole had joined him and was playing the piano to him. She had a pleasant touch, and played Bach and Mozart—both favourite composers of my friend's.

Franklin and Judith came up from the garden about a quarter to one. Judith looked white and strained. She was very silent, looked vaguely about her as though lost in a dream, and then went away. Franklin sat down with us. He, too, looked tired and absorbed, and he had, too, the air of a man very much on edge.

I said, I remember, something about the rain being a relief, and he said quickly:

"Yes. There are times—when *something's* got to break—"

And somehow—I got the impression that it was not merely of the weather that he spoke. Awkward as always in his movements, he jerked against the table and upset half the chocolates. With his usual startled air, he apologized—apparently to the box.

"Oh, sorry."

It ought to have been funny, but somehow it wasn't. He bent quickly and picked up the spilt chocolates.

Norton asked him if he had had a tiring morning.

His smile flashed out then—eager, boyish, very much alive.

"No—no—just realized, suddenly, I've been on the wrong track. Much simpler process altogether is what's needed. Can take a short cut now."

He stood swaying slightly to and fro on his feet, his eyes absent yet resolved.

"Yes, short cut. Much the best way."

III

If we were all nervy and aimless in the morning, the afternoon was unexpectedly pleasant. The sun came out, the temperature was cool and fresh. Mrs. Luttrell was brought down and sat on the verandah. She was in excellent form—exercising her charm and manner with less gush than usual, and with no latent hint of vinegar in reserve. She chaffed her husband, but gently and with a kind of affection, and he beamed at her. It was really delightful to see them on such good terms.

Poirot permitted himself to be wheeled out also,

and he was in good spirits too. I think he liked seeing the Luttrells on such a friendly footing with each other. The Colonel was looking years younger. His manner seemed less vacillating, he tugged less at his moustache. He even suggested that there might be some bridge that evening.

"Daisy here misses her bridge."

"Indeed I do," said Mrs. Luttrell.

Norton suggested it would be tiring for her.

"I'll play one rubber," said Mrs. Luttrell, and added with a twinkle: "And I'll behave myself and not bite poor George's head off."

"My dear," protested her husband, "I know I'm a shocking player."

"And what of that?" said Mrs. Luttrell. "Doesn't it give me grand pleasure badgering and bullying you about it?"

It made us all laugh. Mrs. Luttrell went on:

"Oh, I know my faults, but I'm not going to give them up at my time of life. George has just got to put up with me."

Colonel Luttrell looked at her quite fatuously.

I think it was seeing them both on such good terms that led to a discussion on marriage and divorce that took place later in the day.

Were men and women actually happier by reason of the greater facilities afforded for divorce, or was it often the case that a temporary period of irritation and estrangement—or trouble over a third person—gave way after a while to a resumption of affection and friendliness?

It is odd sometimes to see how much at variance people's ideas are with their own personal experiences.

My own marriage had been unbelievably happy and successful, and I am essentially an old-fashioned person, yet I was on the side of divorce—of cutting one's losses and starting afresh. Boyd Carrington, whose marriage had been unhappy, yet held for an indissoluble marriage bond. He had, he said, the utmost reverence for the institution of marriage. It was the foundation of the state.

Norton, with no ties and no personal angle, was of my way of thinking. Franklin, the modern scientific thinker, was, strangely enough, resolutely opposed to divorce. It offended, apparently, his ideal of clear-cut thinking and action. One assumed certain responsibilities. Those must be carried through and not shirked or set aside. A contract, he said, is a contract. One enters upon it of one's own free will, and must abide by it. Anything else resulted in what he called a mess. Loose ends, half-dissolved ties.

Leaning back in his chair, his long legs kicking vaguely at a table, he said:

"A man chooses his wife. She's his responsibility until she dies—or he does."

Norton said rather comically:

"And sometimes—oh, blessed death, eh?"

We laughed, and Boyd Carrington said:

"You needn't talk, my lad; you've never been married."

Shaking his head, Norton said:

"And now I've left it too late."

"Have you?" Boyd Carrington's glance was quizzical. "Sure of that?"

It was just at that moment that Elizabeth Cole joined us. She had been up with Mrs. Franklin.

I wondered if it was my fancy, or did Boyd Carrington look meaningly from her to Norton, and was it possible that Norton blushed?

It put a new idea into my head and I looked searchingly at Elizabeth Cole. It was true that she was still a comparatively young woman. Moreover, she was quite a handsome one. In fact a very charming and sympathetic person who was capable of making any man happy. And she and Norton had spent a good deal of time together of late. In their hunts for wild flowers and birds, they had become friends; I remembered how she had spoken of Norton being such a kind person.

Well, if so, I was glad for her sake. Her starved and barren girlhood would not stand in the way of her ultimate happiness. The tragedy that had shattered her life would not have been enacted in vain. I thought, looking at her, that she certainly looked much happier and—yes, gayer, than when I had first come to Styles.

Elizabeth Cole and Norton—yes, it might be.

And suddenly, from nowhere, a vague feeling of uneasiness and disquiet assailed me. It was not safe—it was not right—to plan happiness here. There was something malignant about the air of Styles. I felt it now—this minute. Felt suddenly old and tired—yes, and afraid.

A minute later the feeling had passed. Nobody had noticed it, I think, except Boyd Carrington. He said to me in an undertone a few minutes later:

"Anything the matter, Hastings?"

"No, why?"

"Well—you looked—I can't quite explain it."

"Just a feeling—apprehension."

"A premonition of evil?"

"Yes, if you like to put it that way. A feeling that —that something was going to happen."

"Funny. I've felt that once or twice. Any idea what?"

He was watching me narrowly.

I shook my head. For indeed I had had no definite apprehension of any particular thing. It had only been a wave of deep depression and fear.

Then Judith had come out of the house. She had come slowly, her head held high, her lips pressed together, her face grave and beautiful.

I thought how unlike she was to either me or Cinders. She looked like some young priestess. Norton felt something of that too. He said to her:

"You look like your namesake might have looked before she cut off the head of Holofernes."

Judith smiled and raised her eyebrows a little.

"I can't remember now why she wanted to."

"Oh, strictly on the highest moral grounds for the good of the community!"

The light banter in his tones annoyed Judith. She flushed and went past him to sit by Franklin. She said:

"Mrs. Franklin is feeling much better. She wants us all to come up and have coffee with her this evening."

IV

Mrs. Franklin was certainly a creature of moods I thought as we trooped upstairs after dinner. Having made everyone's life unbearable all day, she was now sweetness itself to everybody.

She was dressed in a negligee of pale eau-de-Nil and was lying on her chaise longue. Beside her was a small revolving bookcase-table with the coffee apparatus set out. Her fingers, deft and white, dealt with the ritual of coffee making with some slight aid from Nurse Craven. We were all there with the exception of Poirot, who always retired before dinner; Allerton, who had not returned from Ipswich; and Mrs. and Colonel Luttrell, who had remained downstairs.

The aroma of coffee came to our noses—a delicious smell. The coffee at Styles was an uninteresting muddy fluid, so we all looked forward to Mrs. Franklin's brew with freshly ground berries.

Franklin sat on the other side of the table handing the cups as she filled them. Boyd Carrington stood by the foot of the sofa. Elizabeth Cole and Norton were by the window. Nurse Craven had retired to the background by the head of the bed. I was sitting in an armchair wrestling with the *Times* crossword and reading out the clues.

"Even love—or third party risk?" I read out. "Eight letters."

"Probably an anagram," said Franklin.

We thought for a minute. I went on:

"The chaps between the hills are unkind."

"Tormentor," said Boyd Carrington quickly.

"Quotation: '*And Echo whate'er is asked her answers*'— blank. Tennyson. Five letters."

"Where," suggested Mrs. Franklin. "Surely that's right. 'And Echo answers where'?"

I was doubtful.

"It would make a word end in 'w.' "

"Well, lots of words end in 'w.' *How* and *now* and *snow*."

Elizabeth Cole said from the window:

"The Tennyson quotation is: '*And Echo whate'er is asked her answers Death.*' "

I heard a quick sharp intake of breath behind me. I looked up. It was Judith. She went past us to the window and out upon the balcony.

I said, as I wrote the last clue in: "Even love can't be an anagram. The second letter now is 'A.' "

"What's the clue again?"

"Even love or third party risk. Blank A and six blanks."

"Paramour," said Boyd Carrington.

I heard the teaspoon rattle on Barbara Franklin's saucer. I went on to the next clue.

" 'Jealousy is a green-eyed monster,' this person said."

"Shakespeare," said Boyd Carrington.

"Was it Othello or Emilia?" said Mrs. Franklin.

"All too long. The clue is only five letters."

"Iago."

"I'm *sure* it was Othello."

"It wasn't in *Othello* at all. Romeo said it to Juliet."

We all voiced our opinions. Suddenly from the balcony Judith cried out:

"Look, a shooting star. Oh, there's another."

Boyd Carrington said: "Where? We must wish." He went out on the balcony, joining Elizabeth Cole, Norton and Judith. Nurse Craven went out too. Franklin got up and joined them. They stood there exclaiming, gazing out into the night.

I remained with my head bent over the crossword. Why should *I* wish to see a falling star? I had nothing to wish for . . .

Suddenly Boyd Carrington wheeled back into the room.

"Barbara, you must come out."

Mrs. Franklin said sharply:

"No, I can't. I'm too tired."

"Nonsense, Babs. You must come and wish!" He laughed. "Now don't protest. I'll carry you."

And suddenly stooping, he picked her up in his arms. She laughed and protested:

"Bill, put me down—don't be so silly."

"Little girls have got to come and wish." He carried her through the window and set her down on the balcony.

I bent closer over the paper. For I was remembering . . . A clear tropical night—frogs croaking . . . and a shooting star. I was standing there by the window, and I had turned and picked up Cinders and carried her out in my arms to see the stars and wish . . .

The lines of the crossword ran and blurred before my eyes.

A figure detached itself from the balcony and came into the room—Judith.

Judith must never catch me with tears in my eyes. It would never do. Hastily I swung round the bookcase and pretended to be looking for a book. I remembered having seen an old edition of Shakespeare there. Yes, here it was. I looked through *Othello*.

"What are you doing, Father?"

I mumbled something about the clue, my fingers turning over the pages. Yes, it was Iago.

"O, beware, my lord, of jealousy;
It is the green-eyed monster which doth mock
The meat it feeds on."

Judith went on with some other lines:

"Not poppy, nor mandragora,
Nor all the drowsy syrups of the world,
Shall ever medicine thee to that sweet sleep
Which thou owedst yesterday."

Her voice rang out, beautiful and deep.

The others were coming back, laughing and talking. Mrs. Franklin resumed her place on the chaise longue. Franklin came back to his seat and stirred his coffee. Norton and Elizabeth Cole finished drinking theirs and excused themselves, as they had promised to play bridge with the Luttrells.

Mrs. Franklin drank her coffee and then demanded her "drops." Judith got them for her from the bathroom, as Nurse Craven had just gone out.

Franklin was wandering aimlessly round the room. He stumbled over a small table. His wife said sharply:

"Don't be so clumsy, John."

"Sorry, Barbara. I was thinking of something."

Mrs. Franklin said rather affectedly:

"Such a great bear, aren't you, darling?"

He looked at her rather abstractedly. Then he said:

"Nice night; think I'll take a stroll."

He went out.

Mrs. Franklin said:

"He *is* a genius, you know. You can tell it from

184

his manner. I really do admire him terrifically. Such a passion for his work."

"Yes, yes, clever fellow," said Boyd Carrington—rather perfunctorily.

Judith left the room abruptly, nearly colliding with Nurse Craven in the doorway.

Boyd Carrington said:

"What about a game of picquet, Babs?"

"Oh, lovely. Can you get hold of some cards, Nurse?"

Nurse Craven went to get cards, and I wished Mrs. Franklin good night and thanked her for the coffee.

Outside I overtook Franklin and Judith. They were standing looking out of the passage window. They were not speaking. Just standing side by side.

Franklin looked over his shoulder as I approached. He moved a step or two, hesitated and said:

"Coming out for a stroll, Judith?"

My daughter shook her head.

"Not tonight." She added abruptly, "I'm going to bed. Good night."

I went downstairs with Franklin. He was whistling softly to himself and smiling.

I remarked rather crossly, for I was feeling depressed myself:

"You seem pleased with yourself tonight."

He admitted it.

"Yes. I've done something that I've been meaning to do for a long time. Very satisfactory, that."

I parted from him downstairs and looked in on the bridge players for a minute. Norton winked at me when Mrs. Luttrell wasn't looking. The rubber seemed to be progressing with unusual harmony.

Allerton had still not come back. It seemed to me that the house was happier and less oppressive without him.

I went up to Poirot's room. I found Judith sitting with him. She smiled at me when I came in and did not speak.

"She has forgiven you, *mon ami*," said Poirot—an outrageous remark.

"Really," I spluttered. "I hardly think—"

Judith got up. She put an arm round my neck and kissed me. She said:

"Poor Father. Uncle Hercule shall *not* attack your dignity. *I* am the one to be forgiven. So forgive me and say good night."

I don't quite know why, but I said:

"I'm sorry, Judith. I'm very sorry. I didn't mean—"

She stopped me.

"That's all right. Let's forget it. Everything's all right now." She smiled a slow far-away smile. She said again: "Everything's all right now . . ." and quietly left the room.

When she had gone, Poirot looked at me.

"Well," he demanded, "what has been happening this evening?"

I spread out my hands.

"Nothing has happened or is likely to happen," I told him.

Actually I was very wide of the mark. For something did happen that night. Mrs. Franklin was taken violently ill. Two more doctors were sent for, but in vain. She died the following morning.

It was not until twenty-four hours later that we learned that her death was due to poisoning by physostigmine.

FOURTEEN

The inquest took place two days later. It was the second time I had attended an inquest in this part of the world.

The coroner was an able middle-aged man with a shrewd glance and a dry manner of speech.

The medical evidence was taken first. It established the fact that death was the result of poisoning by physostigmine, and that other alkaloids of the Calabar bean were also present. The poison must have been taken sometime on the preceding evening between seven o'clock and midnight. The police surgeon and his colleague refused to be more precise.

The next witness was Dr. Franklin. He created on the whole a good impression. His evidence was clear and simple. After his wife's death he had checked over his solutions in the laboratory. He had discovered that a certain bottle which should have contained a strong solution of alkaloids of the Calabar bean, with which he had been conducting experiments, had been filled up with ordinary water in which only a trace of the original contents was present. He could not say with certainty when this had been done, as he had not used that particular preparation for some days.

The question of access to the laboratory was then gone into. Dr. Franklin agreed that the laboratory was usually kept locked and that he usually had the key in his pocket. His assistant, Miss Hastings, had a duplicate key. Anyone who wished to go into the studio had to get the key from her or from himself. His wife had borrowed it occasionally, when she had left things belonging to her in the laboratory. He himself had never brought a solution of physostigmine into the house or into his wife's room and he thought that by no possibility could she have taken it accidentally.

Questioned further by the coroner, he said that his wife had for some time been in a low and nervous state of health. There was no organic disease. She suffered from depression and from a rapid alternation of moods.

Of late, he said, she had been cheerful and he had considered her improved in health and spirits. There had been no quarrel between them and they had been on good terms. On the last evening his wife had seemed in good spirits and not melancholy.

He said that his wife had occasionally spoken of ending her life but that he had not taken her remarks seriously. Asked the question definitely, he replied that in his opinion his wife had not been a suicidal type. That was his medical opinion as well as his personal one.

He was followed by Nurse Craven. She looked smart and efficient in her trim uniform, and her replies were crisp and professional. She had been in attendance on Mrs. Franklin for over two months. Mrs. Franklin suffered badly from depression. Witness had heard her say at least three times that she "wanted to end it all," that her life was useless and that she was a millstone round her husband's neck.

"Why did she say that? Had there been any altercation between them?"

"Oh no, but she was aware that her husband had recently been offered an appointment abroad. He had refused that in order not to leave her."

"And sometimes she felt morbidly about the fact?"

"Yes. She would blame her miserable health, and get all worked up."

"Did Dr. Franklin know about this?"

"I do not think she often said so to him."

"But she was subject to fits of depression?"

"Oh, definitely."

"Did she ever specifically mention committing suicide?"

"I think 'I want to end it all' was the phrase she used."

"She never suggested any particular method of taking her own life?"

"No. She was quite vague."

"Had there been anything especially to depress her of late?"

"No. She had been in reasonably good spirits."

"Do you agree with Dr. Franklin that she was in good spirits on the night of her death?"

Nurse Craven hesitated.

"Well—she was excited. She'd had a bad day—complained of pain and giddiness. She had seemed better in the evening—but her good spirits were a bit unnatural. She seemed feverish and rather artificial."

"Did you see anything of a bottle, or anything that might have contained the poison?"

"No."

"What did she eat and drink?"

"She had soup, a cutlet, green peas and mashed potatoes, and cherry tart. She had a glass of Burgundy with it."

"Where did the Burgundy come from?"

"There was a bottle in her room. There was some left afterwards, but I believe it was examined and found to be quite all right."

"Could she have put the drug in her glass without your seeing?"

"Oh yes, easily. I was to and fro in the room, tidying up and arranging things. I was not watching her. She had a little despatch case beside her and also a handbag. She could have put anything in the Burgundy, or later in the coffee, or in the hot milk she had last thing."

"Have you any idea as to what she could have done with the bottle or container if so?"

Nurse Craven considered.

"Well, I suppose she could have thrown it out of the window later. Or put it in the wastepaper basket, or even have washed it out in the bathroom and put it back in the medicine cupboard. There are several empty bottles there. I save them because they come in handy."

"When did you last see Mrs. Franklin?"

"At ten-thirty. I settled her for the night. She had hot milk and she said she'd like an aspirin."

"How was she then?"

The witness considered a minute.

"Well, really, just as usual . . . No, I'd say she was perhaps just a bit overexcited."

"Not depressed?"

"Well, no, more strung-up, so to speak. But if it's suicide you're thinking of, it might make her that way. She might feel noble or exalted about it."

"Do you consider she was a likely person to take her own life?"

There was a pause. Nurse Craven seemed to be struggling to make up her mind.

"Well," she said at last, "I do and I don't. I—yes, on the whole I do. She was very unbalanced."

Sir William Boyd Carrington came next. He seemed genuinely upset, but gave his evidence clearly.

He had played picquet with the deceased on the night of her death. He had not noticed any signs of depression then, but in a conversation some days previously, Mrs. Franklin had mentioned the subject of taking her own life. She was a very unselfish woman, and deeply distressed at feeling that she was hampering her husband's career. She was devoted to her husband and very ambitious for him. She was sometimes very depressed about her own health.

Judith was called, but had little to say.

She knew nothing about the removal of the physostigmine from the laboratory. On the night of the tragedy Mrs. Franklin had seemed to her much as usual, though perhaps overexcited. She had never heard Mrs. Franklin mention suicide.

The last witness was Hercule Poirot. His evidence was given with much emphasis and caused a considerable impression. He described a conversation he had had with Mrs. Franklin on the day previous to her decease. She had been very depressed and had expressed several times a wish to be out of it all. She was worried about her health and had confided in him that she had fits of deep melancholy when life did not seem worth living.

She said that sometimes she felt it would be wonderful to go to sleep and never wake up.

His next reply caused an even greater sensation.

"On the morning of June tenth you were sitting outside the laboratory door?"

"Yes."

"Did you see Mrs. Franklin come out of the laboratory?"

"I did."

"Did she have anything in her hand?"

"She had a small bottle clasped in her right hand."

"You are quite sure of that?"

"Yes."

"Did she show any confusion at seeing you?"

"She looked startled, that is all."

The coroner proceeded to his summing-up. They must make up their minds, he said, how the deceased came to her death. They would have no difficulty in assigning the cause of death, the medical evidence had told them that. Deceased was poisoned by physostigmine sulphate. All they had to decide was whether she took it accidentally or by intent, or if it was administered to her by some other person. They had heard that deceased had fits of melancholy, that she was in poor health, and that while there was no organic disease, she was in a bad nervous condition. M. Hercule Poirot, a witness whose name must carry weight, had asserted positively that he had seen Mrs.

Franklin come out of the laboratory with a small bottle in her hand and that she had seemed startled to see him. They might come to the conclusion that she had taken the poison from the laboratory with the intention of doing away with herself. She seemed to be suffering from an obsession that she was standing in her husband's light and obstructing his career. It was only fair to Dr. Franklin to say that he seemed to have been a kind and affectionate husband, and that he had never expressed annoyance at her delicacy, or complained that she hindered his career. The idea seemed to be entirely her own. Women in a certain condition of nervous collapse did get these persistent ideas. There was no evidence to show at what time, or in what vehicle the poison was taken. It was, perhaps, a little unusual that the bottle which originally contained the poison had not been found, but it was possible that, as Nurse Craven suggested, Mrs. Franklin had washed it and put it away in the bathroom cupboard from where she may have originally taken it. It was for the jury to make their own decision.

The verdict was arrived at after only a short delay.

The jury found that Mrs. Franklin took her own life while temporarily of unsound mind.

II

Half an hour later I was in Poirot's room. He was looking very exhausted. Curtiss had put him to bed and was reviving him with a stimulant.

I was dying to talk, but I had to contain myself until the valet had finished and left the room.

Then I burst out:

"Was that true, Poirot, what you said? That you saw a bottle in Mrs. Franklin's hand when she came out of the laboratory?"

A very faint smile crept over Poirot's bluish-tinged lips. He murmured:

"Did not *you* see it, my friend?"

"No, I did not."

"But you might not have noticed, *hein*?"

"No, perhaps not. I certainly can't swear she didn't have it." I looked at him doubtfully. "The question is, are you speaking the truth?"

"Do you think I would lie, my friend?"

"I wouldn't put it past you."

"Hastings, you shock and surprise me. Where is now your simple faith?"

"Well," I conceded, "I don't suppose you would really commit perjury."

Poirot said mildly:

"It would not be perjury. It was not on oath."

"Then it was a lie?"

Poirot waved his hand automatically.

197

"What I have said, *mon ami*, is said. It is unnecessary to discuss it."

"I simply don't understand you," I cried.

"What don't you understand?"

"Your evidence—all that about Mrs. Franklin's having talked about committing suicide—about her being depressed."

"*Enfin*, you heard her say such things yourself."

"Yes. But it was only one of many moods. You didn't make that clear."

"Perhaps I did not want to."

I stared at him.

"You *wanted* the verdict to be suicide?"

Poirot paused before replying. Then he said:

"I think, Hastings, that you do not appreciate the gravity of the situation. Yes, if you like, I wanted the verdict to be suicide . . ."

"But you don't think—yourself—that she did commit suicide?"

Slowly Poirot shook his head.

I said:

"You think—that she was murdered?"

"Yes, Hastings, she was murdered."

"Then why try to hush it up—to have it labelled and put aside as suicide? That stops all enquiry."

"Precisely."

"You want that?"

"Yes."

"But *why*?"

"Is it conceivable that you do not see? Never mind—let us not go into that. You must take my word for it that it *was* murder—deliberate, pre-conceived murder. I told you, Hastings, that a crime would be committed here, and that it was unlikely we should be able to prevent it—for the killer is both ruthless and determined."

I shivered. I said:

"And what happens next?"

Poirot smiled.

"The case is solved—labelled and put away as suicide. But you and I, Hastings, go on, working underground like moles. And, sooner or later, *we get* X."

I said:

"And supposing that—meanwhile—someone else is killed?"

Poirot shook his head.

"I do not think so. Unless, that is, somebody saw something or knows something—but if so, surely, they would have come forward to say so . . . ?"

FIFTEEN

My memory is a little vague about the events of the days immediately following the inquest on Mrs. Franklin. There was, of course, the funeral, which I may say was attended by a large number of the curious of Styles St. Mary. It was on that occasion that I was addressed by an old woman with rheumy eyes and an unpleasantly ghoulish manner.

She accosted me just as we were filing out of the cemetery.

"Remember you, sir, don't I?"

"Well—er, possibly—"

She went on, hardly listening to what I said.

"Twenty years ago and over. When the old lady died up at the Court. That was the first murder we had to Styles. Won't be the last, I say. Old Mrs.

Inglethorp, her husband done her in, so we all said. Sure of it, we was." She leered at me cunningly. "Maybe it's the husband this time."

"What do you mean?" I said sharply. "Didn't you hear the verdict was suicide?"

"That's what the coroner said. But he might be wrong, don't you think?" She nudged me. "Doctors, they know how to do away with their wives. And she wasn't much good to him seemingly."

I turned on her angrily and she slunk away, murmuring she hadn't meant anything, only it seemed odd-like, didn't it, happening a second time? "And it's queer you should be there both times, sir, isn't it now?"

For one fantastic moment I wondered if she suspected me of having really committed both crimes. It was most disturbing. It certainly made me realize what a queer, haunting thing local suspicion is.

And it was not, after all, so far wrong. For somebody had killed Mrs. Franklin.

As I say, I remember very little of those days. Poirot's health, for one thing, was giving me grave concern. Curtiss came to me with his wooden face slightly disturbed and reported that Poirot had had a somewhat alarming heart attack.

"Seems to me, sir, he ought to see a doctor."

I went posthaste to Poirot, who negatived the suggestion most vigorously. It was, I thought, a little unlike him. He had always been, in my opinion, extremely fussy about his health. Distrusting draughts, wrapping up his neck in silk and wool, showing a horror of getting his feet damp, and taking his temperature and retiring to bed at the least suspicion of a chill—"for otherwise it may be for me a *fluxion de poitrine!*" In most little ailments, he had, I knew, always consulted a doctor immediately.

Now, when he was really ill, the position seemed reversed.

Yet perhaps that was the real reason. Those other ailments *had* been trifling. Now, when he was indeed a sick man, he feared, perhaps, admitting the reality of his illness. He made light of it because he was afraid.

He answered my protests with energy and bitterness.

"Ah, but I have consulted doctors—not one, but many! I have been to Blank and to Dash (he named two specialists) and they do what?—they send me to Egypt where immediately I am rendered much worse. I have been, too, to R."

R. was, I knew, a heart specialist. I asked quickly:

"What did he say?"

Poirot gave me a sudden quick sidelong glance —and my heart gave a sudden agonized leap.

He said quietly:

"He has done for me all that can be done. I have my treatments, my remedies, all close at hand. Beyond that—there is nothing. So you see, Hastings, to call in more doctors would be of no avail. The machine, *mon ami*, wears out. One cannot, alas, install the new engine and continue to run as before like a motor car."

"But look here, Poirot, surely there's something. Curtiss—"

Poirot said sharply: "Curtiss?"

"Yes, he came to me. He was worried— You had an attack—"

Poirot nodded gently.

"Yes, yes. They are, sometimes, these attacks, painful to witness. Curtiss, I think, is not used to these attacks of the heart."

"Won't you really see a doctor?"

"It is of no avail, my friend."

He spoke very gently but with finality. And again my heart felt a painful constriction. Poirot smiled at me. He said:

"This, Hastings, will be my last case. It will be, too, my most interesting case—and my most interesting criminal. For in X we have a technique superb, magnificent—that arouses admiration in spite of oneself. So far, *mon cher*, this X has operated with so much ability that he has defeated me —Hercule Poirot! He has developed the attack to which I can find no answer."

"If you had your health—" I began soothingly.

But apparently that was not the right thing to say. Hercule Poirot immediately flew into a rage.

"Ah! Have I got to tell you thirty-six times, and then again thirty-six, that there is no need of *physical* effort? One needs only—to think."

"Well—of course—yes, you can do that all right."

"All right? I can do it superlatively. My limbs they are paralyzed, my heart it plays me the tricks, but my brain, Hastings—my brain it functions without impairment of any kind. It is still of the first excellence, my brain."

"That," I said soothingly, "is splendid."

But as I went slowly downstairs, I thought to myself that Poirot's brain was not getting on with things as fast as it might do. First the narrow escape of Mrs. Luttrell and now the death of Mrs. Franklin. And what were we doing about it? Practically nothing.

II

It was the following day that Poirot said to me:

"You suggested, Hastings, that I should see a doctor."

"Yes," I said eagerly. "I'd feel much happier if you would."

"*Eh bien,* I will consent. I will see Franklin."

"Franklin?" I looked doubtful.

"Well, he is a doctor, is he not?"

"Yes, but—his main line is research, is it not?"

"Undoubtedly. He would not succeed, I fancy, as a general practitioner. He has not sufficiently what you call the 'side of the bed manner.' But he has the qualifications. In fact I should say that, as the films say, 'he knows his stuff better than most.' "

I was still not entirely satisfied. Although I did not doubt Franklin's ability, he had always struck me as a man who was impatient of and uninterested in human ailments. Possibly an admirable attitude for research work, but not so good for any sick persons he might attend.

However, for Poirot to go so far was a concession, and as Poirot had no local medical attendant, Franklin readily agreed to take a look at him. But he explained that if regular medical attendance was needed, a local practitioner must be called in. He could not attend the case.

Franklin spent a long time with him.

When he came out finally, I was waiting for him. I drew him into my room and shut the door.

"Well?" I demanded anxiously.

Franklin said thoughtfully:

"He's a very remarkable man."

"Oh! That, yes——" I brushed aside this self-evident fact. "But his health?"

"Oh! His health?" Franklin seemed quite surprised—as though I had mentioned something of no importance at all. "Oh! His health's rotten, of course."

It was not, I felt, at all a professional way of putting it. And yet I had heard—from Judith—that Franklin had been one of the most brilliant students of his time.

"How bad is he?" I demanded anxiously.

He shot me a look.

"D'you want to know?"

"Of course."

What did the fool think?

He almost immediately told me:

"Most people," he said, "don't want to know. They want soothing syrup. They want hope. They want reassurance ladled out in driblets. And of course amazing recoveries do occur. But they won't in Poirot's case."

"Do you mean—" Again that cold hand closed round my heart.

Franklin nodded.

"Oh yes, he's for it, all right. And pretty soon, I should say. I shouldn't tell you so if he hadn't authorized me to do so."

"Then—he knows."

Franklin said:

"He knows, all right. That heart of his may go out—phut—any moment. One can't say, of course, exactly *when*."

He paused, then he said slowly:

"From what he says, I gather he's worrying about getting something finished, something that —as he puts it—he's undertaken. D'you know about that?"

"Yes," I said. "I know."

Franklin shot me an interested glance.

"He wants to be sure of finishing off the job."

"I see."

I wondered if John Franklin had any idea of what that job was!

He said slowly:

"I hope he'll manage it. From what he said, it means a lot to him." He paused and added: "He's got a methodical mind."

I asked anxiously:

"Isn't there something that can be done—something in the way of treatment—"

He shook his head.

"Nothing doing. He's got ampoules of amyl nitrite to use when he feels an attack is coming on."

Then he said a rather curious thing.

"Got a very great respect for human life, hasn't he?"

"Yes—I suppose he has."

How often had I not heard Poirot say: "I do not approve of murder." That understatement, made so primly, had always tickled my fancy.

Franklin was going on:

"That's the difference between us. *I* haven't . . . !"

I looked at him curiously. He inclined his head with a faint smile.

"Quite true," he said. "Since death comes anyway, what does it matter if it comes early or late? There's so little difference."

"Then what on earth made you become a doctor if you feel like that?" I demanded with some indignation.

"Oh, my dear fellow—doctoring isn't just a mat-

ter of dodging the ultimate end—it's a lot more
—it's improving *living*. If a healthy man dies, it
doesn't matter—much. If an imbecile—a cretin—
dies, it's a good thing—but if by the discovery of
administering the correct gland you turn your
cretin into a healthy, normal individual by cor-
recting his thyroid deficiency, that, to my mind,
matters a good deal."

I looked at him with more interest. I still felt
that it would not be Dr. Franklin I should call in
if I had the influenza, but I had to pay tribute to
a kind of white-hot sincerity and a very real force
in the man. I had noticed a change in him since
his wife's death. He had displayed few of the conventional signs of mourning. On the contrary he
seemed more alive, less absent-minded, and full
of a new energy and fire.

He said abruptly, breaking into my thoughts:

"You and Judith aren't much alike, are you?"

"No, I suppose we're not."

"Is she like her mother?"

I reflected, then slowly shook my head.

"Not really. My wife was a merry, laughing
creature. She wouldn't take anything seriously—
and tried to make me the same, without much success, I'm afraid."

He smiled faintly.

"No, you're rather the heavy father, aren't you?
So Judith says. Judith doesn't laugh much—serious young woman. Too much work, I expect. My
fault."

He went into a brown study. I said convention-
ally:

"Your work must be very interesting."

"Eh?"

"I said your work must be interesting."

"Only to about half a dozen people. To everybody else it's darned dull—and they're probably
right. Anyway"—he flung his head back, his
shoulders squared themselves, he suddenly looked
what he was, a powerful and virile man—"I've got
my chance now! God, I could shout aloud. The
Minister Institute people let me know today. The
job's still open and I've got it. I start in ten days'
time."

"For Africa?"

"Yes. It's grand."

"So soon." I felt slightly shocked.

He stared at me.

"What do you mean—*soon*? Oh." His brow
cleared. "You mean after Barbara's death? Why
on earth not? It's no good pretending, is it, that
her death wasn't the greatest relief to me?"

He seemed amused by the expression on my
face.

"I've not time, I'm afraid, for conventional atti-
tudes. I fell in love with Barbara—she was a very
pretty girl—married her and fell out of love with
her again in about a year. I don't think it lasted
even as long as that with her. I was a disappointment to her, of course. She thought she could in-

fluence me. She couldn't. I'm a selfish, pigheaded sort of brute, and I do what I want to do."

"But you did refuse this job in Africa on her account," I reminded him.

"Yes. That was purely financial, though. I'd undertaken to support Barbara in the way of life she was accustomed to. If I'd gone, it would have meant leaving her very short. But now"—he smiled a completely frank boyish smile—"it's turned out amazingly lucky for me."

I was revolted. It is true, I suppose, that many men whose wives die are not precisely heartbroken and everyone more or less knows the fact. But this was so blatant.

He saw my face, but did not seem put out.

"Truth," he said, "is seldom appreciated. And yet it saves a lot of time and a lot of inaccurate speech."

I said sharply:

"And it doesn't worry you at all that your wife committed suicide?"

He said thoughtfully:

"I don't really believe she did commit suicide. Most unlikely—"

"But then, what do you think happened?"

He caught me up.

"I don't know. I don't think I—want to know. Understand?"

I stared at him. His eyes were hard and cold. He said again:

"I don't want to know. I'm not—interested. See?"

I didn't see—but I didn't like it.

III

I don't know when it was that I noticed that Stephen Norton had something on his mind. He had been very silent after the inquest, and after that and the funeral were over, he still walked about, his eyes on the ground and his forehead puckered. He had a habit of running his hands through his short grey hair until it stuck up on end like Strumel Peter. It was comical but quite unconscious and denoted some perplexity of his mind. He returned absent-minded answers when you spoke to him, and it did at last dawn upon me that he was definitely worried about something. I asked him tentatively if he had had bad news of any kind, which he promptly negatived. That closed the subject for the time being.

But a little later he seemed to be trying to get an opinion from me on some matter in a clumsy, roundabout way.

Stammering a little, as he always did when he was serious about a thing, he embarked on an involved story centering on a point of ethics.

"You know, Hastings, it should be awfully simple to say when a thing's right or wrong—but really, when it comes to it, it isn't quite such plain

sailing. I mean one may come across something
—the kind of thing, you see, that isn't meant for
you—it's all a kind of accident, and it's the sort
of thing you couldn't take advantage of, and yet
it might be most frightfully important. Do you see
what I mean?"

"Not very well, I'm afraid," I confessed.

Norton's brow furrowed again. He ran his hands
up through his hair again so that it stood upright
in its usual comical manner.

"It's so hard to explain. What I mean is, suppose
you just happened to see something in a private
letter—one opened by mistake, that sort of thing
—a letter meant for someone else and you began
reading it because you thought it was written to
you and so you actually read something you weren't
meant to before you realized. That could happen,
you know."

"Oh yes, of course it could."

"Well, I mean, what would one do?"

"Well—" I gave my mind to the problem. "I
suppose you'd go to the person and say: 'I'm
awfully sorry, but I opened this by mistake.' "

Norton sighed. He said it wasn't quite so simple
as that.

"You see—you might have read something
rather embarrassing, Hastings."

"That would embarrass the other person, you
mean? I suppose you'd have to pretend you hadn't
actually read anything—that you'd discovered
your mistake in time."

"Yes." Norton said it after a moment's pause, and he did not seem to feel that he had yet arrived at a satisfactory solution.

He said rather wistfully:

"I wish I did know what I ought to do."

I said that I couldn't see that there was anything else he could do.

Norton said, the perplexed frown still on his forehead:

"You see, Hastings, there's rather more to it than that. Supposing that what you read was—well, rather important to someone else again, I mean."

I lost patience.

"Really, Norton, I don't see what you do mean. You can't go about reading other people's private letters, can you—"

"No, no, of course not. I didn't mean that. And anyway, it wasn't a letter at all. I only said that to try and explain the sort of thing. Naturally anything you saw or heard or read—by accident—you'd keep to yourself, unless—"

"Unless what?"

Norton said slowly:

"Unless it was something you *ought* to speak about."

I looked at him with suddenly awakened interest. He went on:

"Look here, think of it this way—supposing you saw something through a—a keyhole—"

Keyholes made me think of Poirot! Norton was stumbling on:

"What I mean is, you'd got a perfectly good reason for looking through the keyhole—the key might have stuck and you just looked to see if it was clear—or—or some quite good reason—and you never for one minute expected to see what you did see . . ."

For a moment or two I lost the thread of his stumbling sentences, for enlightenment had come to me. I remembered a day on a grassy knoll and Norton swinging up his glasses to see a speckled woodpecker. I remembered his immediate distress and embarrassment, his endeavours to prevent me from looking through the glasses in my turn. At the moment I had leaped to the conclusion that what he had seen was something to do with *me*—in fact that it was Allerton and Judith. But supposing that that was not the case? That he had seen something quite different? I had assumed that it was something to do with Allerton and Judith because I was so obsessed by them at that time that I could think of nothing else.

I said abruptly:

"Was it something you saw through those glasses of yours?"

Norton was both startled and relieved.

"I say, Hastings, how did you guess?"

"It was that day when you and I and Elizabeth Cole were up on that knoll, wasn't it?"

"Yes, that's right."

"And you didn't want me to see?"

"No. It wasn't—well, I mean it wasn't meant for any of us to see."

"What was it?"

Norton frowned again.

"That's just it. Ought I to say? I mean it was—well, it was spying. I saw something I wasn't meant to see. I wasn't looking for it—there really was a speckled woodpecker—a lovely fellow, and then I saw the other thing."

He stopped. I was curious, intensely curious, yet I respected his scruples.

I asked:

"Was it—something that mattered?"

He said slowly:

"It might matter. That's just it. I don't know."

I asked then:

"Has it something to do with Mrs. Franklin's death?"

He started.

"It's queer you should say that."

"Then it has?"

"No—no, not directly. But it might have." He said slowly: "It would throw a different light on certain things. It would mean that— Oh, damn it all, *I* don't know what to do!"

I was in a dilemma. I was agog with curiosity, yet I felt that Norton was very reluctant to say what he had seen. I could understand that. I should have felt the same myself. It is always unpleasant to come into possession of a piece of information that has been acquired in what the outside world would consider a dubious manner.

Then an idea struck me.

"Why not consult Poirot?"

"Poirot?" Norton seemed a little doubtful.

"Yes, ask his advice."

"Well," said Norton slowly, "it's an idea. Only, of course, he's a foreigner—" He stopped, rather embarrassed.

I knew what he meant. Poirot's scathing remarks on the subject of "playing the game" were only too familiar to me. I only wondered that Poirot had never thought of taking to bird glasses himself! He would have done it if he had thought of it.

"He'd respect your confidence," I urged. "And you needn't act upon his advice if you don't like it."

"That's true," said Norton, his brow clearing. "You know, Hastings, I think that's just what I will do."

IV

I was astonished at Poirot's instant reaction to my piece of information.

"What is that you say, Hastings?"

He dropped the piece of thin toast he had been raising to his lips. He poked his head forward.

"Tell me. Tell me quickly."

I repeated the story.

"He saw something through the glasses that day," repeated Poirot thoughtfully. "Something that he will not tell you." His hand shot out and gripped my arm. "He has not told anyone else of this?"

"I don't think so. No, I'm sure he hasn't."

"Be very careful, Hastings. It is urgent that he should not tell anyone—he must not even hint. To do so might be dangerous."

"Dangerous?"

"Very dangerous."

Poirot's face was grave.

"Arrange with him, *mon ami,* to come up and see me this evening. Just an ordinary friendly little visit, you understand. Do not let anyone else suspect that there is any special reason for his coming. And be careful, Hastings; be very, very careful. Who else did you say was with you at the time?"

"Elizabeth Cole."

"Did she notice anything odd about his manner?"

I tried to recollect.

"I don't know. She may have. Shall I ask her if—"

"You will say nothing, Hastings—absolutely nothing."

SIXTEEN

I gave Norton Poirot's message.

"I'll go up and see him, certainly. I'd like to. But you know, Hastings, I'm rather sorry I mentioned the matter even to you."

"By the way," I said. "You haven't said anything to anyone else about it, have you?"

"No—at least—no, of course not."

"You're quite sure?"

"No, no, I haven't said anything."

"Well, don't. Not until after you've seen Poirot."

I had noticed the slight hesitation in his tone when he first answered, but his second assurance was quite firm. ⹁ was to remember that slight hesitation afterwards, though.

II

I went up again to the grassy knoll where we had been on that day. Someone else was there already. Elizabeth Cole. She turned her head as I came up the slope.

She said:

"You look very excited, Captain Hastings. Is anything the matter?"

I tried to calm myself.

"No, no, nothing at all. I'm just out of breath with walking fast." I added in an everyday commonplace voice:

"It's going to rain."

She looked up at the sky.

"Yes, I think it is."

We stood there silent for a minute or two. There was something about this woman that I found very sympathetic. Ever since she had told me who she really was, and the tragedy that had ruined her life, I had taken an interest in her. Two people who have suffered unhappiness have a great bond in common. Yet for her there was, or so I suspected, a second spring. I said now impulsively:

"Far from being excited, I'm depressed today. I've had bad news about my dear old friend."

"About M. Poirot?"

Her sympathetic interest led me to unburden myself.

When I had finished, she said softly:

"I see. So—the end might come any time?"

I nodded, unable to speak.

After a minute or two I said:

"When he's gone, I shall indeed be alone in the world."

"Oh no, you've got Judith—and your other children."

"They're scattered over the world, and Judith —well, she's got her work. She doesn't need me."

"I suspect that children don't ever need their parents until they are in trouble of some kind. You should make up your mind to that as to some fundamental law. I'm far more lonely than you are. My two sisters are far away—one in America and one in Italy."

"My dear girl," I said. "Your life's beginning."

"At thirty-five?"

"What's thirty-five? I wish I were thirty-five." I added maliciously: "I'm not quite blind, you know."

She turned an enquiring glance on me, then blushed.

"You don't think—oh! Stephen Norton and I are only friends. We've got a good deal in common—"

"All the better."

"He's—he's just awfully kind."

"Oh, my dear," I said. "Don't believe it's all kindness. We men aren't made that way."

But Elizabeth Cole had turned suddenly white. She said in a low, strained voice:

"You're cruel—blind! How can I ever think of —of marriage? With my history. With my sister a murderess—or if not that, insane. I don't know which is worse."

I said strongly:

"Don't let that prey on your mind. Remember, it may not be true."

"What do you mean? It is true."

"Don't you remember saying to me once: 'It wasn't Maggie'?"

She caught her breath.

"One feels like that."

"What one feels is often—true."

She stared at me.

"What do you mean?"

"Your sister," I said, "did not kill her father."

Her hand crept up to her mouth. Her eyes, wide and scared, looked into mine.

"You're mad," she said. "You must be mad. Who told you that?"

"Never mind," I said. "It's true. Someday I'll prove it to you."

III

Near the house I ran into Boyd Carrington.

"This is my last evening," he told me. "I move out tomorrow."

"To Knatton?"

"Yes."

"That's very exciting for you."

"Is it? I suppose it is." He gave a sigh. "Anyway, Hastings, I don't mind telling you, I shall be glad to leave here."

"The food is certainly pretty bad and the service isn't good."

"I don't mean that. After all, it's cheap, and you can't expect much from these paying guest places. No, Hastings, I mean more than discomfort. I don't like this house—there's some malign influence about it. Things happen here."

"They certainly do."

"I don't know what it is. Perhaps a house that has once had a murder in it is never quite the same afterwards . . . But I don't like it. First there was that accident to Mrs. Luttrell—a damned unlucky thing to happen. And then there was poor little Barbara."

He paused.

"The most unlikely person in the world to have committed suicide, *I* should have said."

I hesitated.

"Well, I don't know that I'd go as far as that—"

He interrupted me.

"Well, I would. Hang it all, I was with her most of the day before. She was in good spirits—enjoyed our outing. The only thing she was worrying about was whether John wasn't getting too much wrapped up in his experiments and might overdo things or try some of his messes upon himself. Do you know what I think, Hastings?"

"No."

"That husband of hers is the one who's responsible for her death. Nagged at her, I expect. She was always happy enough when she was with me. He let her see that she handicapped his precious career (I'd give him a career!) and it broke her up. Damned callous, that fellow, hasn't turned a hair. Told me as cool as anything he was off to Africa now. Really, you know, Hastings, I shouldn't be surprised if he'd actually murdered her."

"You don't mean that," I said sharply.

"No—no, I don't really. Though, mind you, mainly because I can see that if he murdered her, he wouldn't do it that way. I mean he was known to be working on this stuff—physostigmine—so it stands to reason if he'd done her in, he wouldn't have used that. But all the same, Hastings, I'm not the only one to think that Franklin's a suspicious character. I had the tip from someone who ought to know."

"Who was that?" I asked sharply.

Boyd Carrington lowered his voice.

"Nurse Craven."

"What?" I was intensely surprised.

"Hush. Don't shout. Yes, Nurse Craven put the idea into my head. She's a smart girl, you know, got her wits about her. She doesn't like Franklin —hasn't liked him all along."

I wondered. I should have said that it was her own patient whom Nurse Craven had disliked. It occurred to me suddenly that Nurse Craven must know a good deal about the Franklin ménage.

"She's staying here tonight," said Boyd Carrington.

"What?" I was rather startled. Nurse Craven had left immediately after the funeral.

"Just for a night between cases," explained Boyd Carrington.

"I see."

I was vaguely disquieted by Nurse Craven's return, yet I could hardly have said why. Was there, I wondered, any reason for her coming back? She didn't like Franklin, Boyd Carrington had said ...

Reassuring myself, I said with sudden vehemence:

"She's no right to hint things about Franklin. After all, it was her evidence that helped to establish suicide. That, and Poirot's seeing Mrs. Franklin coming out of the studio with a bottle in her hand."

Boyd Carrington snapped:

"What's a bottle? Women are always carrying bottles—scent bottles, hair lotion, nail polish. That wench of yours was running about with a bottle in her hand that evening—it doesn't mean *she* was thinking of suicide, does it? Nonsense!"

He broke off as Allerton came up to us. Most appropriately, in melodramatic fashion, there was a low rumble of thunder in the distance. I reflected, as I had reflected before, that Allerton was certainly cast for the part of the villain.

But he had been away from the house on the night of Barbara Franklin's death. And besides, what possible motive could he have had?

But then, I reflected, X never had a motive. That was the strength of his position. It was that, and that only, that was holding us up. And yet, at any minute, that tiny flash of illumination might come.

IV

I think that here and now I should like to place on record that I had never, all through, considered for one moment that Poirot might fail. In the conflict between Poirot and X, I had never contemplated the possibility that X might come out victor. In spite of Poirot's feebleness and ill health, I had faith in him as potentially the stronger of the two. I was used, you see, to Poirot's succeeding.

It was Poirot himself who first put a doubt into my head.

I went in to see him on my way down to dinner. I forget now exactly what led to it, but he suddenly used the phrase "if anything happens to me."

I protested immediately and loudly. Nothing would happen—nothing could happen.

"*Eh bien*, then you have not listened carefully to what Dr. Franklin told you."

"Franklin doesn't know. You're good for many a long year yet, Poirot."

"It is possible, my friend, though extremely unlikely. But I speak now in the particular and not the general sense. Though I may die very soon, it may still be not soon enough to suit our friend X."

"What?" My face showed my shocked reaction. Poirot nodded.

"But yes, Hastings. X is, after all, intelligent. In fact, most intelligent. And X cannot fail to perceive that my elimination, even if it were only to precede natural decease by a few days, might be of inestimable advantage."

"But then—but then—what would happen?" I was bewildered.

"When the colonel falls, *mon ami*, the second in command takes over. You will continue."

"How can I? I'm entirely in the dark."

"I have arranged for that. If anything happens to me, my friend, you will find here"—he patted the locked dispatch case by his side—"all the clues you need. I have arranged, you see, for every eventuality."

"There is really no need to be clever. Just tell me now everything there is to know."

"No, my friend. The fact that you do not know what I know is a valuable asset."

"You have left me a clearly written account of things?"

"Certainly not. X might get hold of it."

"Then what have you left?"

"Indications in kind. They will mean nothing to X—be assured of that—but they will lead you to the discovery of the truth."

"I'm not so sure of that. Why must you have such a tortuous mind, Poirot? You always like making everything difficult. You always have!"

"And it is now with me a passion? Is that what you would say? Perhaps. But rest assured, my indications will lead you to the truth." He paused. Then he said: "And perhaps, then, you would wish that they had not led you so far. You would say instead: *'Ring down the curtain.'*"

Something in his voice started again that vague unformulated dread that I had once or twice felt spasms of already. It was as though somewhere, just out of sight, was a fact that I did not want to see—that I could not bear to acknowledge. Something that already, deep down, *I knew* . . .

I shook the feeling off and went down to dinner.

SEVENTEEN

Dinner was a reasonably cheerful meal. Mrs. Luttrell was down again and in her best vein of artificial Irish gaiety. Franklin was more animated and cheerful than I had yet seen him. Nurse Craven I saw for the first time in mufti instead of her nurse's uniform. She was certainly a very attractive young woman now that she had cast off her professional reserve.

After dinner Mrs. Luttrell suggested bridge, but in the end some round games were started. About half-past nine Norton declared his intention of going up to see Poirot.

"Good idea," said Boyd Carrington. "Sorry he's been under the weather lately. I'll come up too."

I had to act quickly.

"Look here," I said, "do you mind—it really

tires him too much to talk to more than one person at a time."

Norton took the cue and said quickly:

"I promised to lend him a book on birds."

Boyd Carrington said:

"All right. You coming back again, Hastings?"

"Yes."

I went up with Norton. Poirot was waiting. After a word or two I came down again. We began playing rummy.

Boyd Carrington, I think, resented the carefree atmosphere of Styles tonight. He thought, perhaps, that it was too soon after the tragedy for everyone to forget. He was absent-minded, forgot frequently what he was doing, and at last excused himself from further play.

He went to the window and opened it. The sound of thunder could be heard in the distance. There was a storm about, although it had not yet reached us. He closed the window again and came back. He stood for a minute or two watching us play. Then he went out of the room.

I went up to bed at a quarter to eleven. I did not go in to Poirot. He might be asleep. Moreover I felt a reluctance to think any more about Styles and its problems. I wanted to sleep—to sleep and forget.

I was just dropping off when a sound wakened me. I thought it might have been a tap on my door. I called "Come in," but as there was no response, I switched the light on and, getting up, looked out into the corridor.

I saw Norton just coming from the bathroom and going into his own room. He wore a checked dressing gown of particularly hideous colouring and his hair was sticking up on end as usual. He went into his room and shut the door, and immediately afterwards I heard him turn the key in the lock.

Overhead there was a low rumbling of thunder. The storm was coming nearer.

I went back to bed with a slightly uneasy feeling induced by the sound of that turning key.

It suggested, very faintly, sinister possibilities. Did Norton usually lock his door at night? I wondered. Had Poirot warned him to do so? I remembered with sudden uneasiness how Poirot's door key had mysteriously disappeared.

I lay in bed and my uneasiness grew while the storm overhead added to my feeling of nerviness. I got up at last and locked my own door. Then I went back to bed and slept.

II

I went in to Poirot before going down to breakfast.

He was in bed and I was struck again by how ill he looked. Deep lines of weariness and fatigue were on his face.

"How are you, old boy?"

He smiled patiently at me.

"I exist, my friend. I still exist."

"Not in pain?"

"No—just tired," he sighed, "very tired."

I nodded.

"What about last night? Did Norton tell you what he saw that day?"

"He told me, yes."

"What was it?"

Poirot looked at me long and thoughtfully before he replied:

"I am not sure, Hastings, that I had better tell you. You might misunderstand."

"What are you talking about?"

"Norton," said Poirot, "tells me he saw two people—"

"Judith and Allerton," I cried. "I thought so at the time."

"*Eh bien, non. Not* Judith and Allerton. Did I not tell you you would misunderstand? You are a man of one idea!"

"Sorry," I said, a little abashed. "Tell me."

"I will tell you tomorrow. I have much on which I wish to reflect."

"Does it—does it help with the case?"

Poirot nodded. He closed his eyes, leaning back in his pillows.

"The case is ended. Yes, it is ended. There are only some loose ends to be tied. Go down to breakfast, my friend. And as you go, send Curtiss to me."

I did so and went downstairs. I wanted to see Norton. I was deeply curious to know what it was that he had told Poirot.

Subconsciously I was still not happy. The lack of elation in Poirot's manner struck me disagreeably. Why this persistent secrecy? Why that deep inexplicable sadness? What was the *truth* of all this?

Norton was not at breakfast.

I strolled out into the garden afterwards. The air was fresh and cool after the storm. I noticed that it had rained heavily. Boyd Carrington was on the lawn. I felt pleased to see him and wished that I could take him into my confidence. I had wanted to all along. I was very tempted to do so now. Poirot was really unfit to carry on by himself.

This morning Boyd Carrington looked so vital, so sure of himself, that I felt a wave of warmth and reassurance.

"You're up late this morning," he said.

I nodded.

"I slept late."

"Bit of a thunderstorm last night. Hear it?"

I remembered now that I had been conscious of the rolling of thunder through my sleep.

"I felt a bit under the weather last night," said Boyd Carrington. "I feel a lot better today." He stretched his arms out and yawned.

"Where's Norton?" I asked.

"Don't think he's up yet. Lazy devil."

With common accord we raised our eyes. Where we were standing, the windows of Norton's room were just above us. I started. For alone in the façade of windows, Norton's were still shuttered.

I said: "That's odd. Do you think they've forgotten to call him?"

"Funny. Hope he's not ill. Let's go up and see."

We went up together. The housemaid, a rather stupid-looking girl, was in the passage. In answer to a question she replied that Mr. Norton hadn't answered when she knocked. She'd knocked once or twice but he hadn't seemed to hear. His door was locked.

A nasty foreboding swept over me. I rapped loudly on the door, calling as I did so:

"Norton—Norton. Wake up!"

And again with growing uneasiness:

"Wake up . . ."

III

When it was apparent that there was going to be no answer, we went and found Colonel Luttrell. He listened to us with a vague alarm showing in his faded blue eyes. He pulled uncertainly at his moustache.

Mrs. Luttrell, always the one for prompt decisions, made no bones about it.

"You'll have to get that door open somehow. There's nothing else for it."

For the second time in my life, I saw a door broken open at Styles. Behind that door was what had been behind a locked door on the first occasion. *Death by violence.*

Norton was lying on his bed in his dressing gown. The key of the door was in the pocket. In his hand was a small pistol, a mere toy, but capable of doing its work. There was a small hole in the exact centre of his forehead.

For a moment or two I could not think of what I was reminded. Something, surely very old . . .

I was too tired to remember.

IV

As I came into Poirot's room, he saw my face. He said quickly:

"What has happened? Norton?"

"Dead!"

"How? When?"

Briefly I told him.

I ended wearily:

"They say it's suicide. What else can they say? The door was locked. The windows were shuttered. The key was in his pocket. Why! I actually saw him go in and heard him lock the door."

"You saw him, Hastings?"

"Yes, last night."

I explained:

"You're sure it was Norton?"

"Of course. I'd know that awful old dressing gown anywhere."

For a moment Poirot became his old self.

"Ah! But it is a *man* you are identifying, not a *dressing gown*. *Ma foi!* Anyone can wear a dressing gown."

"It's true," I said slowly, "that I didn't see his face. But it was his hair, all right, and that slight limp—"

"Anyone could limp, *mon Dieu!*"

I looked at him, startled.

"Do you mean to suggest, Poirot, that it *wasn't* Norton that I saw?"

"I am not suggesting anything of the kind. I am merely annoyed by the unscientific reasons you give for saying it was Norton. No, no, I do not for one minute suggest that it was *not* Norton. It would be difficult for it to be anyone else, for every man here is tall—very much taller than he was—and *enfin*, you cannot disguise height—that, no. Norton was only five foot five, I should say. *Tout de même*, it is like a conjuring trick, is it not? He goes into his room, locks the door, puts the key in his pocket, and is found shot with the pistol in his hand and the key still in his pocket."

"Then you don't believe," I said, "that he shot himself?"

Slowly Poirot shook his head.

"No," he said. "Norton did not shoot himself. He was deliberately killed."

V

I went downstairs in a maze. The thing was so inexplicable I may be forgiven, I hope, for not seeing the next inevitable step. I was dazed. My mind was not working properly.

And yet it was so logical. Norton had been killed—why? To prevent, or so I believed, his telling what he had seen.

But he had confided that knowledge to one other person.

So that person, too, was in danger . . .

And was not only in danger, but was helpless.

I *should* have known.

I *should* have foreseen . . .

"*Cher ami!*" Poirot had said to me as I left the room.

They were the last words I was ever to hear him say. For when Curtiss came to attend to his master, he found that master dead . . .

EIGHTEEN

I don't want to write about it at all.

I want, you see, to think about it as little as possible. Hercule Poirot was dead—and with him died a good part of Arthur Hastings.

I will give you the bare facts without embroidery. It is all I can bear to do.

He died, they said, of natural causes. That is to say, he died of a heart attack. It was the way, so Franklin said, that he had expected him to go. Doubtless the shock of Norton's death brought one on. By some oversight, it seems, the amyl nitrite ampoules were not by his bed.

Was it an oversight? Did someone deliberately remove them? No, it must have been something more than that. X could not count on Poirot's having a heart attack.

For you see, I refuse to believe that Poirot's death was natural. He was killed, as Norton was killed, as Barbara Franklin was killed. And I don't know *why* they were killed—and I don't know who killed them!

There was an inquest on Norton and a verdict of suicide. The only point of doubt was raised by the surgeon, who said it was unusual for a man to shoot himself in the exact centre of his forehead. But that was the only shadow of a doubt. The whole thing was so plain. The door locked on the inside, the key in the dead man's pocket, the windows closely shuttered—the pistol in his hand. Norton had complained of headaches, it seemed, and some of his investments had been doing badly lately. Hardly reasons for suicide, but they had to put forward something.

The pistol was apparently his own. It had been seen lying on his dressing table twice by the housemaid during his stay at Styles. So that was that. Another crime beautifully stage-managed and as usual with no alternative solution.

In the duel between Poirot and X, X had won.

It was now up to me.

I went to Poirot's room and took away the dispatch box.

I knew that he had made me his executor, so I had a perfect right to do so. The key was round his neck.

In my own room I opened the box.

And at once I had a shock. *The dossiers of X's*

cases were gone. I had seen them there only a day or two previously when Poirot unlocked it. That was proof, if I had been needing it, that X had been at work. Either Poirot had destroyed those papers himself (most unlikely) or else X had done so.

X. X. That damned fiend X.

But the case was not empty. I remembered Poirot's promise that I should find other indications which X would not know about.

Were these the indications?

There was a copy of one of Shakespeare's plays, *Othello*, in a small cheap edition. The other book was the play *John Ferguson* by St. John Ervine. There was a marker in it at the third act.

I stared at the two books blankly.

Here were the clues that Poirot had left for me —and they meant nothing to me at all!

What could they mean?

The only thing I could think of was a code of some kind. A word code based on the plays.

But if so, how was I to get at it?

There were no words, no letters, underlined anywhere. I tried gentle heat with no result.

I read the third act of *John Ferguson* carefully through. A most admirable and thrilling scene where the "wanting" Clutie John sits and talks and which ends with the younger Ferguson going out to seek for the man who has wronged his sister. Masterly character drawing—but I could hardly think that Poirot had left them to improve my taste in literature!

And then, as I turned the leaves of the book over, a slip of paper fell out. It bore a phrase in Poirot's handwriting:

"Talk to my valet Georges."

Well, here was something. Possibly the key to the code, if code it was, had been left with Georges. I must get hold of his address and go to see him.

But first there was the sad business of burying my dear friend.

Here was the spot where he had lived when he first came to this country. He was to lie here at the last.

Judith was very kind to me in these days.

She spent a lot of time with me and helped to make all the arrangements. She was gentle and sympathetic. Elizabeth Cole and Boyd Carrington were very kind, too.

Elizabeth Cole was less affected by Norton's death than I should have thought. If she felt any deep grief, she kept it to herself.

And so it was all ended . . .

II

Yes, I must put it down.
It must be said.

The funeral was over. I was sitting with Judith, trying to make a few sketchy plans for the future. She said then:

"But you see, dear, I shan't be here."

"Not here?"

"I shan't be in England."

I stared at her.

"I haven't liked to tell you before, Father. I didn't want to make things worse for you. But you've got to know now. I hope you won't mind too much. I'm going to Africa, you see, with Dr. Franklin."

I burst out at that. It was impossible. She couldn't do a thing like that. Everyone would be bound to talk. To be an assistant to him in England and especially when his wife was alive was one thing, but to go abroad with him to Africa was another. It was impossible and I was going to forbid it absolutely. Judith must not do such a thing!

She didn't interrupt. She let me finish. She smiled very faintly.

"But, dearest," she said, "I'm not going as his assistant. I'm going as his wife."

It hit me between the eyes.

I said—or rather stammered—"Al-Allerton?"

She looked faintly amused.

"There was never anything in that. I would have told you so if you hadn't made me so angry. Besides, I wanted you to think, well—what you did think. I didn't want you to know it was—John."

"But I saw him kiss you one night—on the terrace."

She said impatiently:

"Oh, I daresay. I was miserable that night. These things happen. Surely you know that?"

I said:

"You can't marry Franklin yet—so soon."

"Yes, I can. I want to go out with him, and you've just said yourself it's easier. We've nothing to wait for—now."

Judith and Franklin. Franklin and Judith.

Do you understand the thoughts that came into my mind—the thoughts that had lain under the surface for some time?

Judith with a bottle in her hand, Judith with her young, passionate voice declaring that useless lives should go to make way for useful ones. Judith whom I loved and whom Poirot also had loved. Those two people that Norton had seen—had they been Judith and *Franklin*? But if so—if so— No, that couldn't be true. Not Judith. Franklin, perhaps—a strange man, a ruthless man, a man who, if he made up his mind to murder, might murder again and again.

Poirot had been willing to consult Franklin.

Why? What had he said to him that morning?

But not Judith. Not my lovely, grave young Judith.

And yet how strange Poirot had looked. How

those words had rung out: "You may prefer to say: '*Ring down the curtain*' . . ."

And suddenly a fresh idea struck me. Monstrous! Impossible! Was the whole story of X a fabrication? Had Poirot come to Styles because he feared a tragedy in the Franklin ménage? Had he come to watch over Judith? Was *that* why he had resolutely told me nothing? Because the whole story of X was a fabrication, a smoke screen?

Was the whole heart of the tragedy Judith, my daughter?

Othello! It was *Othello* I had taken from the bookcase that night when Mrs. Franklin had died. Was that the clue?

Judith that night looking, so someone had said, like her namesake before she cut off the head of Holofernes. Judith—with death in her heart?

NINETEEN

I am writing this in Eastbourne.

I came to Eastbourne to see Georges, formerly Poirot's valet.

Georges had been with Poirot many years. He was a competent, matter-of-fact man, with absolutely no imagination. He always stated things literally and took them at their face value.

Well, I went to see him. I told him about Poirot's death, and Georges reacted as Georges would react. He was distressed and grieved and managed very nearly to conceal the fact.

Then I said:

"He left with you, did he not, a message for me?"

Georges said at once:

"For you, sir? No, not that I am aware of."

I was surprised. I pressed him, but he was quite definite.

I said at last:

"My mistake, I suppose. Well, that's that. I wish you had been with him at the end."

"I wish so, too, sir."

"Still I suppose if your father was ill, you had to come to him."

Georges looked at me in a very curious manner. He said:

"I beg your pardon, sir. I don't quite understand you."

"You had to leave in order to look after your father, isn't that right?"

"I didn't wish to leave, sir. M. Poirot sent me away."

"Sent you away?" I stared.

"I don't mean, sir, that he discharged me. The understanding was that I was to return to his service later. But I left by his wish, and he arranged for suitable remuneration while I was here with my old father."

"But why, Georges, why?"

"I really couldn't say, sir."

"Didn't you ask?"

"No, sir. I didn't think it was my place to do so. M. Poirot always had his ideas, sir. A very clever gentleman, I always understood, sir, and very much respected."

"Yes, yes," I murmured abstractedly.

"Very particular about his clothes, he was—

though given to having them rather foreign and fancy, if you know what I mean. But that, of course, is understandable, as he was a foreign gentleman. His hair, too, and his moustache."

"Ah! Those famous moustaches." I felt a twinge of pain as I remembered his pride in them.

"Very particular about his moustache, he was," went on Georges. "Not very fashionable the way he wore it, but it suited *him*, sir, if you know what I mean."

I said I did know. Then I murmured delicately:

"I suppose he dyed it as well as his hair?"

"He did—er—touch up his moustache a little —but not his hair—not of late years."

"Nonsense," I said. "It was as black as a raven —looked quite like a wig, it was so unnatural."

Georges coughed apologetically.

"Excuse me, sir, it was a wig. M. Poirot's hair came out a good deal lately, so he took to a wig."

I thought how odd it was that a valet knew more about a man than his closest friend did.

I went back to the question that puzzled me.

"But have you really no idea why M. Poirot sent you away as he did? Think, man, *think*."

Georges endeavoured to do so, but he was clearly not very good at thinking.

"I can only suggest, sir," he said at last, "that he discharged me because he wanted to engage Curtiss."

"Curtiss? Why should he want to engage Curtiss."

Georges coughed again.

"Well, sir, I really cannot say. He did not seem to me, when I saw him, as a—excuse me—particularly bright specimen, sir. He was strong physically, of course, but I should hardly have thought that he was quite the class M. Poirot would have liked. He'd been assistant in a mental home at one time, I believe."

I stared at Georges.

Curtiss!

Was that the reason why Poirot had insisted on telling me so little? Curtiss, the one man I had never considered! Yes, and Poirot was content to have it so, to have me combing the guests at Styles for the mysterious X. But X was *not* a guest.

Curtiss!

One-time assistant in a mental home. And hadn't I read somewhere that people who have been patients in mental homes and asylums sometimes remain or go back there as assistants?

A queer, dumb, stupid-looking man—a man who might kill for some strange warped reason of his own . . .

And if so—if so . . .

Why, then a great cloud would roll away from me!

Curtiss—?

POSTSCRIPT

Manuscript written by Hercule Poirot:
  Mon cher ami,
  I shall have been dead four months when you
read these words. I have debated long whether or
not to write down what is written here, and I have
decided that it is necessary for someone to know

the truth about the second "Affaire Styles." Also I hazard a conjecture that by the time you read this you will have evolved the most preposterous theories—and possibly may be giving pain to yourself.

But let me say this: You should, *mon ami*, have easily been able to arrive at the truth. I saw to it that you had every indication. If you have not, it is because, as always, you have far too beautiful and trusting a nature. *A la fin comme au commencement*.

But you should know, at least, who killed Norton—even if you are still in the dark as to who killed Barbara Franklin. The latter may be a shock to you.

To begin with, as you know, I sent for you. I told you that I needed you. That was true. I told you that I wanted you to be my ears and my eyes. That again was true, very true—if not in the sense that you understood it! You were to see what I wanted you to see and hear what I wanted you to hear.

You complained, *cher ami*, that I was "unfair" in my presentation of this case. I withheld from you knowledge that I had myself. That is to say, I refused to tell you the identity of X. That is quite true. I had to do so—though not for the reasons that I advanced. You will see the reason presently.

And now let us examine this matter of X. I showed you the résumé of the various cases. I pointed out to you that in each separate case it seemed quite clear that the person accused, or suspected, had actually committed the crimes in question, that there was no *alternate* solution. And I then proceeded to the second important fact—that in each case X had been either on the scene or closely involved. You then jumped to a deduction that was, paradoxically, both true and false. You said that X had committed all the murders.

But, my friend, the circumstances were such that in each case (or very nearly) *only* the accused person could have done the crime. On the other hand, if so, how account for X? Apart from a person connected with the police force or with, say, a firm of criminal lawyers, it is not reasonable for any man or woman to be involved in five murder cases. It does not, you comprehend, happen! Never, never does it occur that someone says confidentially: "Well, as a matter of fact, I've actually known five murderers"! No, no, *mon ami,* it is not possible, that. So we get the curious result that we have here a case of catalysis—a reaction between two substances that takes place only in the presence of a third substance, that third substance apparently taking no part in the reaction and remaining unchanged. That is the position. It means that where X was present, crimes took place—but X did not actively take part in these crimes.

An extraordinary, an abnormal situation! And I saw that I had come across at last, at the end of my career, the perfect criminal, the criminal who had invented such a technique that *he could never be convicted of crime.*

It was amazing. But it was not new. There were parallels. And here comes in the first of the "clues" I left you. The play of *Othello.* For there, magnificently delineated, we have the original of X. Iago is the perfect murderer. The deaths of Desdemona, of Cassio—indeed of Othello himself—are all Iago's crimes, planned by him, carried out by him. And *he* remains outside the circle, untouched by suspicion—or could have done so. For your great Shakespeare, my friend, had to deal with the dilemma that his own art had brought about. To unmask Iago, he had to resort to the clumsiest of devices—the handkerchief—a piece of work not at all in keeping with Iago's general technique and a blunder of which one feels certain he would not have been guilty.

Yes, there is there the perfection of the art of murder. Not even a word of *direct* suggestion. He is always holding back others from violence, refuting with horror suspicions that have not been entertained until he mentions them!

And the same technique is seen in the brilliant third act of *John Ferguson*—where the "half-witted" Clutie John induces others to kill the man that he himself hates. It is a wonderful piece of psychological suggestion.

Now you must realize this, Hastings. Everyone is a potential murderer—in everyone there arises from time to time the *wish* to kill—though not the *will* to kill. How often have you not felt or heard others say: "She made me so furious I felt I could have killed her!" "I could have killed B. for saying so-and-so!" "I was so angry I could have murdered him!" And all those statements are literally true. Your mind at such moments is quite clear. You would like to kill so-and-so. *But you do not do it.* Your will has to assent to your desire. In young children, the brake is as yet acting imperfectly. I have known a child, annoyed by its kitten, say: "Keep still or I'll hit you on the head and kill you" and actually do so—to be stunned and horrified a moment later when it realizes that the kitten's life will not return—because, you see, really the child loves that kitten dearly. So then, we are all potential murderers. And the art of X was this: not to suggest the *desire*, but to break down the normal decent resistance. It was an art perfected by long practice. X knew the exact word, the exact phrase, the intonation even to suggest and to bring cumulative pressure on a weak spot! It could be done. It was done without the victim ever suspecting. It was not hypnotism—hypnotism would not have been successful. It was something more insidious, more deadly. It was a marshalling of the forces of a human being to widen a breach instead of repairing it. It called on the best in a man and set it in alliance with the worst.

You should know, Hastings—for it happened to you . . .

So now, perhaps, you begin to see what some

of my remarks that annoyed and confused you really meant. When I spoke of a crime to be committed, I was not always referring to the same crime. I told you that I was at Styles for a purpose. I was there, I said, because a crime was going to be committed. You were surprised at my certainty on that point. But I was able to be certain—for the crime, you see, was to be committed *by myself* . . .

Yes, my friend, it is odd—and laughable—and terrible! I, who do not approve of murder—I, who value human life—have ended my career by committing murder. Perhaps it is because I have been too self-righteous, too conscious of rectitude—that this terrible dilemma had to come to me. For you see, Hastings, there are two sides to it. It is my work in life to save the innocent—to *prevent* murder—and this—this is the only way I can do it! Make no mistake. X could not be touched by the law. He was safe. By no ingenuity that I could think of could he be defeated any other way.

And yet, my friend—I was reluctant. I saw what had to be done—but I could not bring myself to do it. I was like Hamlet—eternally putting off the evil day . . . And then the next attempt happened—the attempt on Mrs. Luttrell.

I had been curious, Hastings, to see if your well-known flair for the obvious would work. It did. Your very first reaction was a mild suspicion of Norton. And you were quite right. Norton was the man. You had no reason for your belief—except the perfectly sound if slightly half-hearted suggestion that he was insignificant. There, I think, you came very close to the truth.

I have considered his life history with some care. He was the only son of a masterful and bossy woman. He seems to have had at no time any gift for asserting himself or for impressing his personality on other people. He has always been slightly lame and was unable to take part in games at school.

One of the most significant things you told me was a remark about him having been laughed at at school for nearly being sick when seeing a dead rabbit. There, I think, was an incident that may have left a deep impression on him. He disliked blood and violence and his prestige suffered in consequence. Subconsciously, I should say, he has waited to redeem himself by being bold and ruthless.

I should imagine that he began to discover quite young his own power for influencing people. He is a good listener, he has a quiet, sympathetic personality. People liked him without, at the same time, noticing him very much. He resented this—and then made use of it. He discovered how ridiculously easy it was, by using the correct words and supplying the correct stimuli, to influence his fellow creatures. The only thing necessary was to understand them—to penetrate their thoughts, their secret reactions and wishes.

Can you realize, Hastings, that such a discovery might feed a sense of power? Here was he, Stephen Norton, whom everyone liked and despised—and he could make people do things they didn't want to do—or (mark this) thought they did not want to do.

I can visualize him developing this hobby of his . . . And little by little developing a morbid taste for violence at second hand. The violence for which he lacked physical stamina and for the lack of which he had been derided.

Yes, his hobby grows and grows until it comes to be a passion, a necessity! It was a drug, Hastings—a drug that induced craving as surely as opium or cocaine might have done.

Norton, the gentle-natured loving man, was a secret sadist. He was an addict of pain, of mental torture. There has been an epidemic of that in the world of late years—*L'appétit vient en mangeant*.

It fed two lusts—the lust of the sadist and the lust of power. He, Norton, had the keys of life and of death.

Like any other drug slave, he had to have his supply of the drug. He found victim after victim. I have no doubt there have been more cases than the five I actually tracked down. In each of those he played the same part. He knew Etherington, he stayed one summer in the village where Riggs lived and drank with Riggs in the local pub. On a cruise he met the girl Freda Clay and encouraged and played upon her half-formed conviction that if her old aunt died it would be really a good thing—a release for Auntie and a life of financial ease and pleasure for herself. He was a friend of the Litchfields and when talking to him, Margaret Litchfield saw herself in the light of a heroine delivering her sisters from their life sentence of imprisonment. But I do not believe, Hastings, that any of these people would have done what they did—but for Norton's influence.

And now we come to the events at Styles. I had been on Norton's track for some time. He became acquainted with the Franklins and at once I scented danger. You must understand that even Norton has to have a nucleus on which to work. You can only develop a thing of which the seed is already present. In *Othello,* for instance, I have always been of the belief that already present in Othello's mind was the conviction (possibly correct) that Desdemona's love for him was the passionate unbalanced hero worship of a young girl for a famous warrior and not the balanced love of a *woman* for Othello the *man.* He may have realized that Cassio was her true mate and that in time she would come to realize the fact.

The Franklins presented a most agreeable prospect to our Norton. All kinds of possibilities! You have doubtless realized by now, Hastings (what anyone of sense could have seen perfectly plainly all along), that Franklin was in love with Judith and she with him. His brusqueness, his habit of never looking at her, of forsaking any attempt at courtesy, ought to have told you that the man was head over ears in love with her. But Franklin is a man of great strength of character and also of great rectitude. His speech is brutally unsentimental, but he is a man of very definite standards. In his code a man sticks to the wife he has chosen.

Judith, as I should have thought even you could have seen, was deeply and unhappily in love with him. She thought you had grasped the fact that day you found her in the rose garden. Hence her furious outburst. Characters like hers cannot stand any expression of pity or sympathy. It was like touching a raw wound.

Then she discovered that you thought it was Allerton she cared for. She let you think so, thereby shielding herself from clumsy sympathy and from a further probing of the wound. She flirted with Allerton as a kind of desperate solace. She knew exactly the type of man he was. He amused her and distracted her, but she never had the least feeling for him.

Norton, of course, knew exactly how the wind lay. He saw possibilities in the Franklin trio. I may say that he started first on Franklin, but drew a complete blank. Franklin is the one type of man who is quite immune from Norton's kind of insidious suggestion. Franklin has a clear-cut, black and white mind, with an exact knowledge of his own feeling—and a complete disregard for outside pressure. Moreover, the great passion of his life is his work. His absorption in it makes him far less vulnerable.

With Judith, Norton was far more successful.
He played very cleverly on the theme of useless
lives. It was an article of faith with Judith—and
the fact that her secret desires were in accordance
with it was a fact that she ignored stridently while
Norton knew it to be an ally. He was very clever
about it—taking himself the opposite point of
view, gently ridiculing the idea that she would
ever have the nerve to do such a decisive action.
"It is the kind of thing that all young people say
—but never do!" Such an old cheap jibe—and
how often it works, Hastings! So vulnerable they
are, these children! So ready, though they do not
recognize it that way, to take a dare!

And with the useless Barbara out of the way,
then the road is clear for Franklin and Judith.
That was never said—that was never allowed to
come into the open. It was stressed that the *personal* angle had nothing to do with it—nothing
at all. For if Judith once recognized that it had,
she would have reacted violently. But with a murder addict so far advanced as Norton, one iron in
the fire is not enough. He sees opportunities for
pleasure everywhere. He found one in the Luttrells.

Cast your mind back, Hastings. Remember the
very first evening you played bridge. Norton's
remarks to you afterwards, uttered so loud that
you were afraid Colonel Luttrell would hear. Of
course! Norton meant him to hear! He never lost
an opportunity of underlining it—rubbing it in.

And finally his efforts culminated in success. It happened under your nose, Hastings, and you never saw how it was done. The foundations were already laid—the increasing sense of a burden borne, of shame at the figure he cut in front of other men, in a deep growing resentment against his wife.

Remember exactly what happened. Norton says he is thirsty. (Did he know Mrs. Luttrell is in the house and will come upon the scene?) The Colonel reacts immediately as the open-handed host which he is by nature. He offers drinks. He goes to get them. You are all sitting outside the window. His wife arrives—there is the inevitable scene—which he knows is being overheard. He comes out. It might have been glossed over by a good pretence —Boyd Carrington could have done it well. (He has a certain amount of worldly wisdom and a tactful manner—though otherwise he is one of the most pompous and boring individuals that I have ever come across! Just the sort of man you would admire!) You yourself could have acquitted yourself not too badly. But Norton rushes into speech, heavily, fatuously, underlining tact until it screams to heaven and makes things much worse. He babbles of bridge (more recalled humiliations), talks aimlessly of shooting accidents. And prompt on his cue, just as Norton intended, that old woolly-headed ass Boyd Carrington comes out with his story of an Irish batman who shot his brother—a story, Hastings, that *Norton told to Boyd Carrington,* knowing quite well that the old fool would bring it out as his own whenever suitably prompted. You see, the supreme suggestion will not come from Norton. *Mon Dieu, non!*

It is all set, then. The cumulative effect. The breaking point. Affronted in his instincts as a host —shamed before his fellow men, writhing under the knowledge that they are quite convinced he has not got the guts to do anything but submit meekly to bullying—and then the key words of escape. The rook rifle, accidents—man who shot his brother—and suddenly, bobbing up, his wife's head . . . "Quite safe—an accident . . . *I'll* show them . . . I'll show *her* . . . damn her! I wish she was dead . . . She *shall* be dead!"

He did not kill her, Hastings. Myself, I think that, even as he fired, instinctively he missed *because he wanted to miss.* And afterwards—afterwards the evil spell was broken. She was his wife, the woman he loved in spite of everything.

One of Norton's crimes that did not quite come off.

Ah, but his next attempt! Do you realize, Hastings, that it was *you* who came next? Throw your mind back—recall everything. *You,* my honest, kindly Hastings! He found every weak spot in your mind—yes, and every decent and conscientious one, too.

Allerton is the type of man you instinctively dislike and fear. He is the type of man that you think ought to be abolished. And everything you heard about him and thought about him was true. Norton tells you a certain story about him—an entirely true story as far as the facts go. (Though actually the girl concerned was a neurotic type and came of poor stock.)

It appeals to your conventional and somewhat old-fashioned instincts. This man is the villain, the seducer, the man who ruins girls and drives them to suicide! Norton induces Boyd Carrington to tackle you also. You are impelled to "speak to Judith." Judith, as could be predicted, immediately responds by saying she will do as she chooses with her life. That makes you believe the worst.

See now the different stops on which Norton plays. Your love for your child. The intense old-fashioned sense of responsibility that a man like you feels for his children. The slight self-importance of your nature. "*I* must do something. It all depends on *me*." Your feeling of helplessness owing to the lack of your wife's wise judgment. Your loyalty—I must not fail her. And, on the baser side, your vanity—through association with me you have learned all the tricks of the trade! And lastly, that inner feeling which most men have about their daughters—a father's unreasoning jealousy and dislike for the man who takes his daughter away from him. Norton played, Hastings, like a virtuoso on all these tunes. And you responded.

You accept things too easily at their face value. You always have done. You accepted quite easily the fact that it was Judith to whom Allerton was talking in the summerhouse. Yet you did not see her, you did not even hear her speak. And incredibly, even the next morning, you still thought it was Judith. You rejoiced because she had "changed her mind."

But if you had taken the trouble to examine the facts, you would have discovered at once that there had never been any question of Judith going up to London that day! And you failed to make another most obvious inference. There was someone who was going off for the day—and who was furious at not being able to do so. Nurse Craven. Allerton is not a man who confines himself to the pursuit of one woman! His affair with Nurse Craven had progressed much further than the mere flirtation he was having with Judith.

No, stage management again by Norton.

You saw Allerton and Judith kiss. Then Norton shoves you back round the corner. He doubtless knows quite well that Allerton is going to meet Nurse Craven in the summerhouse. After a little argument he lets you go but still accompanies you. The sentence you overhear Allerton speaking is magnificent for his purpose and he swiftly drags you away before you have a chance to discover that the woman is not Judith!

Yes, the virtuoso! And your reaction is immediate, complete on all those themes! You responded. You made up your mind to do murder.

But fortunately, Hastings, you had a friend

whose brain still functioned. And not only his brain!

I said at the beginning of this that if you have not arrived at the truth, it is because you have too trusting a nature. You believe what is said to you. You believed what *I* said to you . . .

Yet it was all very easy for you to discover the truth. I had sent Georges away—why? I had replaced him with a less experienced and clearly much less intelligent man—why? I was not being attended by a doctor—I, who have always been careful about my health—I would not hear of seeing one—why?

Do you see now why you were necessary to me at Styles? I had to have someone who accepted what I said without question. You accepted my statement that I came back from Egypt much worse than when I went. I did not. I came back very much better! You could have found out the fact if you had taken the trouble. But no, you believed. I sent away Georges because I could not have succeeded in making him think that I had suddenly lost all power in my limbs. Georges is extremely intelligent about what he sees. He would have known that I was shamming.

Do you understand, Hastings? All the time that I was pretending to be helpless and deceiving Curtiss, I was not helpless at all. I could walk—with a limp.

I heard you come up that evening. I heard you hesitate and then go into Allerton's room. And at once I was on the alert. I was already much exercised about your state of mind.

I did not delay. I was alone. Curtiss had gone down to supper. I slipped out of my room and across the passage. I heard you in Allerton's bathroom. And promptly, my friend, in the manner you so much deplore, I dropped to my knees and looked through the keyhole of the bathroom door. One could see through it, fortunately, as there is a bolt and not a key on the inside.

I perceived your manipulations with the sleeping tablets. I realized what your idea was.

And so, my friend, I acted. I went back to my room. I made my preparations. When Curtiss came up, I sent him to fetch you. You came, yawning and explaining that you had a headache. I made at once the big fuss—urged remedies on you. For the sake of peace you consented to drink a cup of chocolate. You gulped it down quickly so as to get away quicker. But I, too, my friend, have some sleeping tablets.

And so, you slept—slept until morning, when you awoke your own sane self and were horrified at what you had so nearly done.

You were safe now—one does not attempt these things twice—not when one has relapsed into sanity.

But it decided *me*, Hastings! For whatever I might not know about other people did not apply to you. *You* are not a murderer, Hastings! But you might have been hanged for one—for a murder committed by another man who in the eyes of the law would be guiltless.

You, my good, my honest, my oh-so-honourable Hastings—so kindly, so conscientious—so innocent!

Yes, I must act. I knew that my time was short —and for that I was glad. For the worst part of murder, Hastings, is its effect on the murderer. I, Hercule Poirot, might come to believe myself divinely appointed to deal out death to all and sundry . . . But mercifully, there would not be time for that to happen. The end would come soon. And I was afraid that Norton might succeed with someone who was unutterably dear to us both. I am talking of your daughter . . .

And now we come to the death of Barbara Franklin. Whatever your ideas may be on the subject, Hastings, I do not think you have once suspected the truth.

For you see, Hastings, *you* killed Barbara Franklin.

Mais oui, you did!

There was, you see, yet another angle to the triangle. One that I did not fully take into account. As it happened, Norton's tactics there were unseen and unheard by either of us. But I have no doubt that he employed them . . .

Did it ever enter your mind to wonder, Hastings, why Mrs. Franklin was willing to come to Styles? It is not, when you think of it, at all her line of country. She likes comfort, good food and above all social contacts. Styles is not gay—it is not well run—it is in the dead country. And yet it was Mrs. Franklin who insisted on spending the summer there.

Yes, there was a third angle—Boyd Carrington. Mrs. Franklin was a disappointed woman. That was at the root of her neurotic illness. She was ambitious both socially and financially. She married Franklin because she expected him to have a brilliant career.

He was brilliant, but not in her way. His brilliance would never bring him newspaper notoriety or a Harley Street reputation. He would be known to half a dozen men of his own profession and would publish articles in learned journals. The outside world would not hear of him—and he would certainly not make money.

And here is Boyd Carrington—home from the East—just come into a baronetcy and money, and Boyd Carrington has always felt tenderly sentimental towards the pretty seventeen-year-old girl he nearly asked to marry him. He is going to Styles, he suggests the Franklins come too—and Barbara comes.

How maddening it is for her! Obviously she has lost none of her old charm for this rich, attractive man—but he is old-fashioned—not the type of man to suggest divorce. And John Franklin, too, has no use for divorce. If John Franklin were to die—then she could be Lady Boyd Carrington—and oh, what a wonderful life that would be!

CURTAIN

Norton, I think, found her only too ready a tool.

It was all too obvious, Hastings, when you come to think of it. Those first few tentative attempts at establishing how fond she was of her husband. She overdid it a little—murmuring about "ending it all" because she was a drag on him.

And then an entirely new line. Her fears that Franklin might experiment upon himself.

It ought to have been so obvious to us, Hastings! She was preparing us for John Franklin to die of physostigmine poisoning. No question, you see, of anyone trying to poison him—oh no—just pure scientific research. He takes the harmless alkaloid, and it turns out to be harmful after all.

The only thing was it was a little too swift. You told me that she was not pleased to find Boyd Carrington having his fortune told by Nurse Craven. Nurse Craven was an attractive young woman with a keen eye for men. She had had a try at Dr. Franklin and had not met with success. (Hence her dislike for Judith.) She is carrying on with Allerton—but she knows quite well he is not serious. Inevitable that she should cast her eye on the rich and still attractive Sir William. And Sir William was, perhaps, only too ready to be attracted. He had already noticed Nurse Craven as a healthy, good-looking girl.

Barbara Franklin has a fright and decides to act quickly. The sooner she is a pathetic, charming and not inconsolable widow, the better.

And so, after a morning of nerves, she sets the scene.

Do you know, *mon ami*, I have some respect for the Calabar bean. This time, you see, it worked. It spared the innocent and slew the guilty.

Mrs. Franklin asks you all up to her room. She makes coffee with much fuss and display. As you tell me, her own coffee is beside her, her husband's on the other side of the bookcase table.

And then there are the shooting stars and everyone goes out and only you, my friend, are left— you and your crossword puzzle and your memories—and to hide emotion, you swing round the bookcase to find a quotation in Shakespeare.

And so they come back and Mrs. Franklin drinks the coffee full of the Calabar bean alkaloids that were meant for dear scientific John, and John Franklin drinks the nice plain cup of coffee that was meant for clever Mrs. Franklin.

But you will see, Hastings, if you think a minute, that although I realized what had happened, I saw that there was only one thing to be done. I could not *prove* what had happened. And if Mrs. Franklin's death was thought to be anything but suicide, suspicion would inevitably fall on either Franklin or Judith. On two people who were utterly and completely innocent. So I did what I had a perfect right to do—laid stress on, and put conviction into, my repetition of Mrs. Franklin's extremely unconvincing remarks on the subject of putting an end to herself.

I could do it—and I was probably the only person who could. For you see my statement carried weight. I am a man experienced in the matter of committing murder. If *I* am convinced it is suicide, well then, it will be accepted as suicide.

It puzzled you, I could see, and you were not pleased. But mercifully you did not suspect the true danger.

But will you think of it after I am gone? Will it come into your mind, lying there like some dark serpent that now and then raises its head and says: "Suppose Judith . . . ?"

It may do. And therefore I am writing this. You must know the truth.

There was one person whom the verdict of suicide did not satisfy. Norton. He was balked, you see, of his pound of flesh. As I say, he is a sadist. He wants the whole gamut of emotion, suspicion, fear, the coils of the law. He was deprived of all that. The murder he had arranged had gone awry.

But presently he saw what one may call a way of recouping himself. He began to throw out hints. Earlier on he had pretended to see something through his glasses. Actually he intended to convey the exact impression that he did convey—namely, that he saw Allerton and Judith in some compromising attitude. But not having said anything definite, he could use that incident in a different way.

Supposing, for instance, that he says he saw *Franklin* and Judith. That will open up an inter-

esting new angle of the suicide case! It may, perhaps, throw doubts on whether it was suicide . . .

So, *mon ami*, I decided that what had to be done
must be done at once. I arranged that you should
bring him to my room that night . . .

I will tell you now exactly what happened. Norton, no doubt, would have been delighted to tell
me his arranged story. I gave him no time. I told
him, clearly and definitely, all that I knew about
him.

He did not deny it. No, *mon ami*, he sat back
in his chair and smirked. *Mais oui*, there is no
other word for it—he smirked. He asked me what
I thought I was going to do about this amusing
idea of mine. I told him that I proposed to execute
him.

"Ah," he said, "I see. The dagger or the cup of
poison?"

We were about to have chocolate together at the
time. He has a sweet tooth, M. Norton.

"The simplest," I said, "would be the cup of
poison."

And I handed him the cup of chocolate I had
just poured out.

"In that case," he said, "would you mind my
drinking from your cup instead of from mine?"

I said: "Not at all." In effect, it was quite im-
material. As I have said, I, too, take the sleeping
tablets. The only thing is that since I have been
taking them every night for a considerable period,

I have acquired a certain tolerance, and a dose that would send M. Norton to sleep would have very little effect upon me. The dose was in the chocolate itself. We both had the same. His portion took effect in due course, mine had little effect upon me, especially when counteracted with a dose of my strychnine tonic.

And so to the last chapter. When Norton was asleep, I got him into my wheelchair—fairly easy, it has many types of mechanism—and wheeled him back in it to its usual place in the window embrasure behind the curtains.

Curtiss then "put me to bed." When everything was quiet, I wheeled Norton to his room. It remained, then, to avail myself of the eyes and ears of my excellent friend Hastings.

You may not have realized it, but I wear a wig, Hastings. You will realize even less that I wear a false moustache. (Even Georges does not know that!) I pretended to burn it by accident soon after Curtiss came, and at once had my hairdresser make me a replica.

I put on Norton's dressing gown, ruffled up my grey hair on end, and came down the passage and rapped on your door. Presently you came and looked with sleepy eyes into the passage. You saw Norton leave the bathroom and limp across the passage into his own room. You heard him turn the key in the lock on the inside.

I then replaced the dressing gown on Norton,

laid him on his bed, and shot him with a small pistol that I acquired abroad and which I have kept carefully locked up except for two occasions when (nobody being about) I have put it ostentatiously on Norton's dressing table, he himself being well away somewhere those mornings.

Then I left the room after putting the key in Norton's pocket. I myself locked the door from the outside with the duplicate key which I have possessed for some time. I wheeled the chair back to my room.

Since then I have been writing this explanation.

I am very tired—and the exertions I have been through have strained me a good deal. It will not, I think, be long before . . .

There are one or two things I would like to stress.

Norton's were the perfect crimes.

Mine was not. It was not intended to be.

The easiest way and the best way for me to have killed him was to have done so quite openly—to have had, shall we say, an accident with my little pistol. I should have professed dismay, regret—a most unfortunate accident. They would have said: "Old ga-ga didn't realize it was loaded—*ce pauvre vieux.*"

I did not choose to do that.

I will tell you why.

It is because, Hastings, I chose to be "sporting." *Mais oui*, sporting! I am doing all the things that so often you have reproached me with not doing. I am playing fair with you. I am giving you a run for your money. I am playing the game. You have every chance to discover the truth.

In case you disbelieve me, let me enumerate all the clues.

The keys.

You know, for I have told you so, that Norton arrived here *after* I did. You know, for you have been told, that I changed my room after I got here. You know, for again it has been told to you, that since I have been at Styles, the key of my room disappeared and I had another made.

Therefore when you ask yourself: Who could have killed Norton? Who could have shot and still have left the room (apparently) locked on the inside since the key is in Norton's pocket? The answer is: "Hercule Poirot, who since he has been here has possessed duplicate keys of one of the rooms."

The man you saw in the passage.

I myself asked you if you were sure the man you saw in the passage was Norton. You were startled. You asked me if I intended to suggest it was *not* Norton. I replied, truthfully, that I did not at all intend to suggest it was not Norton. (Naturally, since I had taken a good deal of trouble to suggest it *was* Norton.) I then brought up the question of *height*. All the men, I said, were much taller than Norton. But there *was* a man who was shorter than Norton—Hercule Poirot. And it is comparatively easy with raised heels or elevators in the shoes to add to one's height.

You were under the impression that I was a helpless invalid. But why? Only because *I said so*. And I had sent away Georges. That was my last indication to you, "Go and talk to Georges."

Othello and Clutie John show you that X was Norton.

Then who could have killed Norton?

Only Hercule Poirot.

And once you suspected that, everything would have fallen into place—the things I had said and done, my inexplicable reticence. Evidence from the doctors in Egypt, from my own doctor in London, that I was not incapable of walking about. The evidence of Georges as to my wearing a wig. The fact which I was unable to disguise, and which you ought to have noticed, that I limp much more than Norton does.

And last of all, the pistol shot. My one weakness. I should, I am aware, have shot him through the temple. I could not bring myself to produce an effect so lopsided, so haphazard. No, I shot him symmetrically, in the exact centre of the forehead ...

Oh, Hastings, Hastings! *That* should have told you the truth.

But perhaps, after all, you *have* suspected the truth? Perhaps when you read this, you already *know*.

But somehow I do not think so . . .

No, you are too trusting . . .

You have too beautiful a nature . . .

What shall I say more to you? Both Franklin and Judith, I think you will find, knew the truth although they will not have told it to you. They will be happy together, those two. They will be poor, and innumerable tropical insects will bite them and strange fevers will attack them—but we all have our own ideas of the perfect life, have we not?

And you, my poor lonely Hastings? Ah, my heart bleeds for you, dear friend. Will you, for the last time, take the advice of your old Poirot?

After you have read this, take a train or a car or a series of buses and go to find Elizabeth Cole, who is also Elizabeth Litchfield. Let her read this, or tell her what is in it. Tell her that you, too, might have done what her sister Margaret did— only for Margaret Litchfield there was no watchful Poirot at hand. Take the nightmare away from her, show her that her father was killed, not by his daughter, but by that kind sympathetic family friend, that "honest Iago," Stephen Norton.

For it is not right, my friend, that a woman like that, still young, still attractive, should refuse life because she believes herself to be tainted. No, it is not right. Tell her so, you, my friend, who are yourself still not unattractive to women . . .

Eh bien, I have no more now to say. I do not

know, Hastings, if what I have done is justified or not justified. No—I do not know. I do not believe that a man should take the law into his own hands . . .

But on the other hand, I *am* the law! As a young man in the Belgian police force I shot down a desperate criminal who sat on a roof and fired at people below. In a state of emergency martial law is proclaimed.

By taking Norton's life, I have saved other lives —innocent lives. But still I do not know . . . It is perhaps right that I should not know. I have always been so sure—too sure . . .

But now I am very humble and I say like a little child: "I do not know . . ."

Good-bye, *cher ami*. I have moved the amyl nitrite ampoules away from beside my bed. I prefer to leave myself in the hands of the *bon Dieu*. May his punishment, or his mercy, be swift!

We shall not hunt together again, my friend. Our first hunt was here—and our last . . .

They were good days.

Yes, they have been good days. . . .

End of Hercule Poirot's manuscript.

(Final note by Captain Arthur Hastings:
I have finished reading . . . I can't believe it all yet . . . But he is right. I should have known. I should have known when I saw the bullet hole so symmetrically in the middle of the forehead.

CURTAIN

Queer—it's just come to me—the thought in the back of my mind that morning.

The mark on Norton's forehead—it was like the brand of Cain. . . .)